THE DREAM

THE DREAM

Iain Crichton Smith

MACMILLAN
LONDON

First published 1990 by
MACMILLAN LONDON LIMITED
4 Little Essex Street London WC2R 3LF
and Basingstoke

Reprinted 1990

Associated companies in Auckland, Delhi, Dublin, Gaborone,
Hamburg, Harare, Hong Kong, Johannesburg, Kuala Lumpur, Lagos,
Manzini, Melbourne, Mexico City, Nairobi, New York, Singapore and Tokyo

A CIP catalogue record for this book is available from the British Library.

ISBN 0-333-52190-0

Typeset by Matrix, 21 Russell Street, London WC2

Printed in Great Britain by
Billing & Sons Ltd, Worcester

F or a whole week before he made his final decision Martin was unable to speak; he completely lost his voice. It was quite extraordinary, nothing like it had happened to him before. It forced him to study the world around him in a quite new way. He would have to point to objects instead of casually mentioning them. Instead of shouting to Jean from one room to another he would have to leave the room he was in and communicate his message visually.

But the oddest thing was that objects began to overwhelm him. He would stare at a vase or a yellow bedspread and see them as they were without a name. And because they had no names which he could communicate they were much more themselves than they ordinarily were: they were more present, more urgent. It was as if the very function of language, by labelling the objects, could make them less important; one could easily pass them by like long familiar members of a family. But to imagine them struggling into language, to see them as shapeless and diffuse, was a different thing altogether.

Even Jean became more present to him, not simply as a name, but as a being. Her dark hair, her slightly rounded face, her legs which were more muscular than she liked – these impinged on him in

1

a new way. Her quick, busy walk became even more urgent. It was as if he were looking at someone who, though not exactly strange, had clicked into focus in a startlingly novel illumination, which brought her into close-up.

It was, he found, eerie to be walking about or sitting in that silence. The TV, when it was on, seemed louder, its diurnal and nocturnal chatter more irrelevant. Jean's movements became like those of an actress in a silent film. The noises of the city outside were louder, more magnified, more enigmatic. He became more and more conscious of language itself, of the many languages going on around him. It was as if he was at bay in a silent castle of his own.

He wanted to tell Jean this but couldn't, precisely because he couldn't speak. And then again she didn't arrive home till after five and for most of the day he was alone since there was no point in going to the university. The silence of the house was oppressive. In it he could hear the click made occasionally by the refrigerator, or the noises made by the walls themselves. He would walk about the rooms touching the furniture as if to say, You at least are here. I love your continuity, I can depend on you.

Sometimes, if he concentrated, he could hear a kind of roar all about him, as if things were desperately trying to attain language and therefore individuality; as if a huge wardrobe were thrusting its gigantic mahogany towards him for attention. (It was a wardrobe he had inherited from his old home on the island, and, though Jean didn't like it, he wished to keep it, and against her protests had done so.)

But oh, that silence, how it troubled him. He would clear his throat now and again to see if his voice had returned to him. And even the attempt was in itself an intrusion upon the silence around him. He would gargle, drink coffee – as if perhaps he thought that the warmth would help him to speak again. But all that week it was as if he had determined to be silent. And from the streets outside the cries of children floated in through the open window. The curtains billowed like ghosts into the air. Various smells entered. But still he was alone in a more real sense than he had been before. Once or twice he had the idea that Jean would not return from her work, and he would rush to the phone to talk to her only to realise speech was impossible. He imagined her telling a customer about Austria, about Switzerland, opening a brochure, pointing to a timetable, a map, and then he felt absolutely desolated and helpless.

He also had nightmares. Normally he could never remember his dreams when he woke in the clear light of morning, but one in particular he recalled vividly. He was rowing across a dark stream to the further bank. When he arrived people were there, but he found that he couldn't speak to them. There was something he wished to say to them, some message he had to give them, but he couldn't tell them what it was, for no matter how volubly he spoke they didn't seem to understand. After a while, he stared down at his clothes and saw spots of red appearing on them. The natives, for such they appeared to be, gabbled furiously at each other, now and again pointing to the blood and then discussing him among themselves, glancing sideways at him with secret, almost mocking looks. The message, whatever it was, seemed urgent, but he could never transmit it and this made him angrier and angrier and more despairing. He woke from these dreams sweating and silent, unable to tell Jean about them – Jean who sat up startled in the bed in her white nightgown, like a ghost.

'I think', he said to Jean, when he had his voice back again, 'I shall go back to the island.'

It came as a tremendous shock to her. She turned on him furiously, 'What?'

'I've been thinking about it,' he said. 'The fact is, my life at the moment is a contradiction.'

'Go on.'

'Well, look at it,' he went on. 'Here I am in the middle of Glasgow teaching Gaelic when the language itself is dying on the islands. Can't you see it's a contradiction?'

'Let it die,' she said, in the same furious, venomous voice.

'You mean you don't care?'

'No, I don't care.' Her lips trembled as if she were about to cry.

'But can't you see the position I'm in? Here I am researching Gaelic in the middle of a city which on the whole doesn't know any. It's like . . . ' He paused. 'It's completely nonsensical, absurd. It's like a barber having a shop among a lot of bald people.'

She glanced at his balding pate and smiled a little.

'If the language is going to be saved it must be saved at the source. I've given it a lot of thought. I want to give up my lectureship and take a teaching job on the island.'

'And lose pay?'

'Yes, I would lose pay. I can't deny that.'

'We don't have any children,' she said, with apparent irrelevance.

'No, we don't. Will you come with me?' he said tenderly.

'No.'

It was only at that moment that he realised his decision had a finality which perhaps he hadn't quite bargained for. She was, he could now see, absolutely determined not to return to the island. If he had ever thought that she had got over all that, he could now disillusion himself.

'I think,' she said, standing up, 'that I'll go for a walk.'

'Now? It's seven o'clock.'

'It doesn't matter. It's safe enough, though people say it isn't. I've never seen any violence here.'

'If that's what you want.'

'No, it's not what I want,' she said. 'I'll tell you something. Things haven't been well between us for a long time. You know that.'

He was stunned. 'I don't know what you're talking about. I really don't.' But then women, as much as the island, had always puzzled him.

'Think about it,' she said.

When Nina, their neighbour, heard that he hadn't been well, she called on them. She lived next door – had left the island many years before – but her husband who had been a policeman had died and now she only went there on holidays.

At a certain stage in the evening she became maudlin and reminiscent. Sitting up on the green sofa she said, 'I would go back tomorrow if I could. But of course we don't even have a croft there now. What is there for me in Glasgow? I sit for hours at the window.'

'But you go to the *ceilidhs*,' said Jean, who was sitting on a chair near the fire, her legs crossed.

'I know that, but that's only in the winter-time. I miss John. I miss him all the time.'

John had been a big, red-necked, slow-pacing policeman who had never been promoted but had been popular.

She sipped her vodka. 'The days of our youth,' she said. 'The open doors. Do you remember, Martin? They never locked the doors. There was never any stealing.'

Martin didn't like that kind of talk. It made the islanders out to be exceptional, which they weren't. They were like other human beings, except that they had a language of their own. He drank his whisky morosely and listened, watching her face reddening with nostalgia and drink in the reflection from the firelight.

'When I go back now it's all different,' she said. Jean glanced at Martin as if to say, I told you so. He avoided her eye. 'The people are different,' she said. 'Even in the shops the girls are rude. They have no time to talk to you. People don't cut the peats. And it's all TV, just as here. At one time there was the community, you see.'

Any moment now she might sing, 'Nuair a Bha Sinn Og' ('When We Were Young').

'Yes,' she said. 'I came with John to the big city when I was young. It nearly broke my heart. But I like the Glasgow people now.'

Jean waited for Martin to speak, but he didn't say anything. He let Nina run on like a river, which she was willing to do: her visit was really an excuse to reminisce and drink vodka. The slight moustache above her lips seemed to quiver with a life of its own.

She seemed to him to be a caricature of all that he despised about the islanders' love of their past. God, he thought, how complicated everything is, this snake winding around me. Sometimes I feel that I cannot speak at all, that there is nothing I can say.

'It's like going back to a strange place,' she continued. 'It's not like home any longer. I don't know anyone. There's a coldness. And do you know this, hardly any of the young ones speak the language? If you speak to them in Gaelic they answer in English.'

She turned her blind red sad face towards him. He remembered a poem which compared such a face to a stopped clock.

'Did you hear that, Martin?' said Jean. She had been drinking more than usual, he could see. Normally she hardly drank at all.

'I heard,' he said. 'That's precisely one more reason why . . . ' And he stopped. He hated himself for using the word 'precisely'. It was a lecturer's word, and he had almost ceased to think of himself as a lecturer.

Nina continued, ignoring the two of them. 'They don't even have their own cows now. They get their milk from the mainland.'

And, at that moment, Martin saw again the vague blue hills, the cows coming heavily home in the twilight, and himself drinking the warm milk.

'Imagine that,' said Nina. 'Just imagine it. And no horses either. In the old days we cut the peats as a community, everybody helped everybody else, no money changed hands. Now they have the electricity and coal just like ourselves.' She shook her head despairingly.

And why not? thought Martin. Why shouldn't they have coal and electricity 'just like ourselves'?

7

Why should they cut peat if they didn't want to? In order to give Nina her dreams?

And why weren't the three of them speaking Gaelic to each other in this room? Jean, of course, wouldn't speak Gaelic to him. She had condemned the island to silence. There like a triangle, it stood in the middle of the sea, finished with – a geometrical figure. Why wasn't Nina speaking Gaelic then? Was it because she thought of him as a lecturer and therefore her social superior? He smiled.

Sure enough, Nina was singing to herself,

'Feasgar agus ceò ann
's mi Steòrnabhagh nan sràd . . . '*

He despised that sort of song. It was pop, that was all it was. There were certain Gaelic songs and singers he despised tremendously.

Jean defiantly poured herself another glass of wine. He knew that she would be sick later, she couldn't take much drink. He drank his own whisky neat.

Let me look into that island as into a mirror. What can I see? The lochs of my childhood, the midges hovering about them, the trout, the purple hills in the background, the heather . . .

Why wouldn't the woman go? But Nina sat there mistily in her vague nostalgia as if she would never leave. There was no reason why she couldn't sell her house and return to the island if she wanted to. But deep down she didn't want to, it was as simple as that. And she blamed the island for changing, and not herself. So many excuses . . .

*An evening with mist I was in Stornoway of the streets . . .

But she did eventually go, clasping the two of them in her arms at the door and singing, 'Goodbye and a good night to you,' as they did at the end of *ceilidhs*. They watched her walk slightly unsteadily down their path and turn right in the Glasgow night into her own house. Jean was sick, as he had expected: her bile was as green as the water round the shore of the island. She clasped herself round him as they lay in bed. In her sleep she kept saying, 'Don't go, don't go.'

The fact was that Jean thought of Martin's returning to the island as a sort of divorce. It was as if she considered the island as a woman able to corrupt and entice him. The island was her rival. Martin couldn't understand why she thought like that since he had never been unfaithful to her. He had always loved her. But her thoughts were not like his; they were rooted in a different consciousness. He couldn't explain to her the deadness that came over him during his lectures, the feeling that he was a hypocrite, that somehow or other he was not living an authentic life. What was the point of teaching Old Irish and Welsh, when his own language was dying at home?

'You don't care about people,' she would say to him. 'All you care about is your language.'

She was better with people than he was, much better. Perhaps that came from working in the travel agency where she consulted brochures and directed customers to Australia, Canada, Hawaii, and many other places. There were five of them in the office altogether, four girls and a man – Smith his name was. Martin had seen him once or twice; he was quite young and shy.

Jean would come home with little stories from

the office. She told him of the couple who came back from a London tour on which an American had said, after the guide had informed him that the Magna Carta had been signed in 1015, 'Gosh, we're fifteen minutes late.' And other tales of this kind, nearly all about Americans in Italy, or Greece, or London.

When she first started work in the office she had been very naïve having travelled hardly anywhere except Aberdeen. Her innocence was a delight to him, as were her anecdotes. Now, however, she was much more sophisticated; perhaps his scholarly silences had infected her. Before they were married they had chattered to each other a great deal (in cars, hotels, restaurants, cinemas) but after marriage the silences had become lengthy. Sometimes, he could not think of anything to talk to her about since she was not particularly interested in the Gaelic poets he studied. (Why should she be?) It was as if he had frozen a babbling childish brook, and nevertheless he expected it to be what it had always been. On the other hand, when she turned to a newspaper and was silent in her turn, he resented it.

And had he frozen her? Did he think that his studies were so important? – that he was dealing with men of talent, scrutinising their utterances, analysing their poetic devices, comparing them with each other with greater exactness than she compared various butters, cheeses, steaks in the supermarket?

But at least she had her own work. She sat in her office and sent people to all corners of the world; told them of prices, routes, coinage, cities, foods, climates and so on, expected them to enjoy themselves, to be changed, was glad to be helping them, advising them. Sent them to countries which had different languages – languages they couldn't understand though they could make themselves understood. Bravely they went into that ignorance, bravely they searched among the strange words, and bravely enjoyed themselves. The glamour of Hong Kong, Indonesia, India, the lights of green and red, the curious fish caught in the warm seas, the mysterious Orient.

She got on well with everybody really. With her workmates in the office, to whom she talked about babies, nights out, romances, straying husbands, houses, gardens . . . in other words, that was her language.

She lived in the centre of an enchanted web of journeys, voyages, maps, charts, seas, while beside her and around her she was anchored to the reality of Glasgow, its diurnal affairs.

The dream, thought Martin, here they are searching for the dream. The audience is dreaming its communal dream in the middle of Glasgow in a bu'lding which stands beside an Indian restaurant called the Eastern Star, while the big red buses splash past with their transparent cages of people. They're dreaming of the Isle of Skye, Tiree, Mull – the jewels in the sea, dim and sonorous, which sound behind their lives even in the city. The *ceilidh* is a method of stabilising time, of freezing it, of returning to the ideal dream of childhood when the moons shone over the autumn cornfields, over the ghostly stooks. The dream is what makes the city bearable.

There are two thousand people here. They sit quietly in their seats as the chairman in his kilt and black velvet jacket stands up, says a few words

11

in Gaelic and then continues in English, surrounded by his platform party all of them in tartan.

And now here, as singer after singer stands up and sings verse after verse of an anglified song, dressed in long tartan skirt or kilt, he is astounded. How different from the *ceilidhs* of the past when a house in the village was chosen and people sat around the fire telling stories of the day or of the past, singing songs in an intimate atmosphere, not on a platform, not fixed in this artificial format, so formal and ludicrous.

> ' . . . where I was reared when young
> where there are the peatstacks . . . '

sang the singer. What is the meaning of this? thought Martin, glancing around him at the captivated audience. Here are those who have their work in Glasgow, who every morning stream to their offices on the underground, on buses, in cars, sinuous as a snake; here they are lost in the dream of the imagination, refreshed at those waterholes, sleeping the sleep of the exile, and yet apparently awake with their handbags in their hands, their half-bottles in their hip-pockets, in the middle of the swarming city, the still threatening city, children again.

And what is this doing for the language? he thought, as he had so often before. What is this sleep doing for the language which needs to be alive, to be searching out new roads, new paths, new strategies? What are these garishly dressed rainbow people doing for the language?

> ' . . . the isle of Scalpay, of Harris,
> the beautiful isle of my love . . . '

12

sang the singer. The words bathed the audience in a world that was long past; they recalled the lark singing in the morning, the wells from which they drew the water before pipes were laid down, the walks in the purple evening, the moon 'of the ripening of the barley', the dancing at the corner of the road in the open air to the music of the melodeon.

At the interval Martin went outside for a breath of fresh air. The buses swayed past him, the lights from the Indian restaurant, green and red, glittered in the pools of water. The lights themselves were a pulsing, active language – the language of the city; the lights above the cinema two doors away announced the arrival of E.T. from outer space.

A drunk young man came up to him and spoke in Gaelic. Martin answered in Gaelic. The young man offered him a swig from a half-bottle he was carrying, and Martin accepted it. The young man put his arms around him and began to sing. He told him that he was in the Merchant Navy and in port for a few days. He had been to New Zealand on his latest voyage.

'It's a great thing to hear the Gaelic,' he said. He sang, his arms around Martin,

> 'When I climb to her masts
> I cannot see the hills of Lewis . . . '

There were tears in his eyes; he swayed, carrying Martin with him through the pools where the lights from the Indian restaurant were reflected and together they composed a drunken, wavering dance.

> 'Sweetheart, do you remember
> the night before I sailed . . . '

13

Martin could have sworn that he saw the letters E.T. reflected in the coloured water. The young man, whose name turned out to be Angus, swayed happily. He loved Martin, Martin was his friend. Martin should have been with him in Auckland, there was no place better than Auckland. If he chose a place other than his island in which to settle down it would be Auckland; he had nearly jumped the ship in New Zealand. He had met John Macdonald there – did Martin know John Macdonald? – John Macdonald hadn't written home for years, he had met him in a pub at the docks, he and John Macdonald had a great night together, talking of the old days. John Macdonald . . .

Did Martin want to go back to the hall? Why didn't they go to a pub together and have a singsong? He knew a good pub, he always went to it whenever he came to Glasgow . . .

'. . . Whenever I go to Jamaica Street
    there will be a man and a woman on each corner . . . '

Martin had a dream as they swayed together in their drunken, chained dance. The lights in the pool were a Celtic script; he was reading Gaelic poems as red as blood. A police car passed with its blue light pulsing, followed by an ambulance. An accident somewhere, said a part of his mind . . .

The young drunken man didn't want to stay in Glasgow; he would return to his island, he would take over the croft if it hadn't been sold, he would marry. He hadn't married yet – how could he marry? How could he support a wife and children on the island? Especially now with the fishing the way it was, the trawlers overfishing the grounds, and he

14

didn't want an office job, that was for sure. What did Martin think? and he raised a blubbery face towards him. Martin didn't know. Go on, he thought, sail the seven seas, that at least would be better than sitting in this dream: it would be better to see New Zealand than an Isle of Mull that never existed.

The drunk young man was now muttering to himself, lost in a dream of melancholia, speaking words that Martin couldn't hear, half-words such as he saw on a shop in front of him where some of the letters were missing from a name and composed a word which might have been Hungarian or Polish.

He managed to disengage himself from the drunk and strode briskly through the Glasgow night in which a thin rain was falling.

Jean wouldn't have his mother down with them when she was dying.

'No,' she said, 'she wouldn't be happy here. And I'm working and you're working. Do you want me to give up my job?'

'I wouldn't want that,' said Martin.

'Well, then.'

And so his mother had to go into hospital and he imagined her thinking, Look at all I've done for him and this is what happens.

Yet wasn't Jean right? Her own mother had died when young, and as for her aunt who had brought her up, she too had died of cancer (not that Jean was sorry about that).

'The fact is there comes a point when you have to lead your own life,' said Jean. 'Anything else is sentiment.'

It was true of course. If his mother had come

to live with them, then Jean would have to give up her job. And then his mother might have died in a month, a year, and it wouldn't be easy for Jean to get another job. When you looked at it like that, it was manifestly logical. And yet . . .

After all, his mother had been very kind to him. He remembered her standing in the kitchen baking, flour on her hands, in a kitchen much smaller than the one he and Jean had in Glasgow where there were labelled jars for tea, coffee, sugar, cinnamon, rice and so on. The kitchen was the biggest room in the house.

But on the island there had been an oilcloth on the table and in the early years a Tilley lamp casting its globe of light. At that kitchen table he had studied when he was in secondary school, secure while his mother was sewing or knitting. She never read; he was the one who did the reading. How proud she had been when he had become a lecturer.

And there she was in the hospital wondering why he hadn't taken her to the security of his own home. But Jean wouldn't hear of it.

'It's common sense,' she said. 'She's hardly ever left the island. She would hate Glasgow. Even in the hospital there will be people she knows, nurses, patients.'

But . . . the still, small voice spoke to Martin.

His mother's flowery dress, like a summer pasture, billowed out of the past. He hadn't even been there when she died, six months exactly after she had been taken to the hospital. And now his older brother, still unmarried, had the croft.

His grief had been tremendous. He had shouted at Jean in a fever of guilt and conscience. And Jean had stood strongly out against him.

'It was necessary,' she said. 'It wouldn't have

16

worked. Anyway, she never liked me, you know that. She hated me for taking her "boy" away from her. Perhaps she wanted you to be unmarried as well?'

And he had got drunk and staggered through the streets of Glasgow, seeing in front of him her flowered dress in the yellow light, as if she were a phantom that he was pursuing, his youth, his precious youth.

'She had so little,' he said to Jean, blubbering. 'Her husband died before her. We were never rich. So little. And look at all we have.' And he had smashed some of the earthenware jars against the wall, shouting, 'Look at this kitchen. It is as big as a tomb.'

But still Jean stood out against him, and in spite of himself he admired her for her strength as she picked up the fragments of jars, as if from an archaeology expedition that had just passed.

'It was her or me,' she said. 'That is the fact. She would have tried to split us up, I know it. It would have been natural. And, another thing, she would have insisted on speaking Gaelic and you know I don't like the language. Little things she would have done.'

Next day she had replaced the earthenware jars: Martin found them ranged as before when he returned from the funeral. The coffin had been taken to the cemetery near the sea. It had been a lovely day with the grass shifting slightly in the wind, the waves glittering in the bay. No one had said anything about his inhumanity, his lack of filial care, but he had felt a disapproval. Everyone had been kind to him as the coffin was lowered into the hole in the sandy earth. His hair had risen slightly like the grass, there were shadows dancing on the tombstones which leaned away from the self-delighting sea. He had shaken his brother's hand, taken the plane back, tied the

17

belt around himself, and watched the white clouds through the window like a downy pillow on which he might rest, like the flour which had mapped her dress. Jean had been waiting for him at the airport. She looked composed, solid yet pale. She was his only comfort now. His mother would fade and change but Jean would remain his wife, whom he had taken in sickness and in health.

'I have no regrets,' she said, 'and you should have none either. You used to send her money. She would have split us up. She would have done terrible harm,' she said, as she swerved to avoid a big van that towered almost on top of them, loaded with wood. 'When you think about it you'll know I was right.'

I sit or sometimes perch on a desk in this lecture room and I talk to them about Irish mythology, about grammar, about words. Cuchulain I tell them about, Naoise and Deirdre, the *Book of Deer*, the book of the Dean of Lismore, the poems which the monks wrote sitting in their gardens with the plants blossoming and the birds twittering, and I tell them about the *Book of Kells* with its enamelled designs. The P people and the Q people I tell them about, the Brythonic and the Goidelic. And they sit and listen and take notes. And what will happen to them? Will they go back like missionaries to the islands, will there be jobs for them? And all the time I am telling them this, the language on the islands is dying, the well is drying up. And what am I doing here, this walking, sitting paradox that I am?

Some of the other lecturers do not notice this; they are quite happy to be studying genealogies, philology, to be adding a footnote to a poem or a piece of prose, to be unearthing a letter that a poet wrote to his tailor a hundred years ago, to be translating, comparing. Yet far from here the language is dying.

And he would perch like a bird on the edge of a desk and listen to the noise of the city. I am tired of genealogies, of grammar, of philology. I have been doing it too long; I ache for the sound of real talk, of language as it is lived, of some reality that I am missing. My mind is here, but where is the rest of me? My mind sees the P and Q people streaming in from Europe, alighting in Wales, in the Highlands, in Ireland, in Cornwall, talking in their sodden huts, but where is that passion, that emotion I should be feeling? I am a head with roots in it. I am like a turnip in the middle of the city, glaring and blue and phantasmal. And to this city my people came many years ago, to its clocks, to its new urgent rhythms, in their new clothes, to their factories, to their gas-lit stairs. It was to this city, not to philologies, not to roots, but to shipyards, to dim, damp closes, to factories.

And on one girl he gazed while she bent over her notebook, her fine, fair hair shining in the light, one who was older than the others, one who wished to go to teach in the islands when she had finished her university studies, one who sat like a nun in front of him, studious, shy, who herself wrote some poems which she had shown him, distant, aloof, attractive like the island itself.

Her name was Gloria Summers.

This is the story of Jean.

When her mother was nineteen years old she went to a dance which was held after a football match. There she met a footballer who was playing in one of the teams while home on leave from the navy. Let it be imagined that she drank more than she was accustomed to, that he was intense and demanding because of his fear and his glory (since he had scored one of the most important goals that had given victory to his team), that he was importunate and passionate and that she loved him for his glory and pitied him for the possible death that he might suffer. Imagine that he was also more experienced and older than she, that it was a summer night with the fragrance and wandering mysteries of June, and that she surrendered herself like a white fish to his net (actually he was to drown in the Atlantic and be devoured by fishes four months later). And that she became pregnant, to deliver her child when the father was dead; she never told anyone who he was. And though he promised to write to her he never did. So the baby milked her and the father drowned in a sea he hardly knew. And all the time she was carrying the baby she was frightened and alone; she became paler and paler, she would weep for no reason. Her parents would ask her what was wrong, and when the baby came they turned away from her towards their church and the house became a marble house, for they were religious people, and she forgot the glory and majesty of summer and thought of that night as the point where she was impaled on death, though the baby was healthy and cried lustily.

In those days the island was besieged by tuberculosis. Patients were hiding shamefully in houses, not wishing to go to the sanatorium where so many died since there was no cure. They spat out their milky spittle, and faded away like candles from which the wax falls. And the shame of TB and the shame of the illegitimate child came together and she contracted the disease herself, as if she wanted to expiate her sin. She lay in the sanatorium whitening and thinning and coughing, while the sister who was the true flower of her religious parents looked after the child – not to be taken to the sanatorium in case it too contracted the tubercular germ, for TB was a plague that stalked the islands and in its thin hooded face there was no mercy.

And so she died, still young, and the child grew up with the aunt who never knew that the lover was lolling about in the Atlantic, though the child did discover later from a neighbour that it might have been such and such, the famous footballer, as the neighbour herself had been at that summer dance years ago. But the child grew up, twice doomed, first because of her illegitimacy and second because of the sin that stalked the island.

She was told about her illegitimacy: no, it was not kept from her, and her mother was hardly ever mentioned in the house, for not even her sacrificial death had saved her. Oh, how she had to kneel in the evenings against the sofa to listen to her aunt or her uncle reading a passage from the Bible preceded by a psalm and followed by a prayer. How around her on the wall were photographs of ministers like film stars. How she had to attend Sunday school neatly dressed. How she was called in on a Sunday if she tried to play. How she sought private solace for herself in that house over which the wings of sin hovered.

She crept about since she was not a real person. She was told of the deceit of men, of the terrible lies that passion generated, she was shown the emotions as her enemies. And even her sudden impulses of joy, so natural to childhood, her spurts towards love, were repelled as if they were infections which had to be guarded against at all costs.

Her aunt wore black, sat upright at the table, and told her stories about hell, about what happened to those who strayed from the correct road, brought her up as best she could in the 'true ways'.

And in spite of that the child rebelled. She would shout and scream, she would beat with her buckled shoe on the floor, she would fight this dreadful blackness as if she were being slowly drowned and was beating with all her strength against the sea, and sometimes in her hysterical rages not even the aunt would be able to control her. Sometimes she would shout at her, 'I hate you, I hate you,' and once tried to run away, only to be brought back by a neighbour from a haystack where she had been sheltering from the pouring rain.

And at night in her bed she would weep and devise ways of killing her aunt with phantom knives, since she recognised that in spite of her protestations of help she was her enemy, her true enemy, the witch who tormented her.

And there came a time in her teens when she said that there was no God, and was belted mercilessly by her uncle who was calm and slow and methodical in his punishment. And though she didn't believe in God she believed in Christ, for at least there were lambs she could cuddle and protect, and Christ himself was said to have been a lamb.

Hell however poured towards her in eternal fire; she had nightmares, she would wake from her bed screaming, she would wet her bed and be punished for it. She was no one, being illegitimate. She had to learn that her aunt had done everything for her, that her mother had been a fallen woman. There were no photographs of her in the house; she had been wiped away much as a dictatorial regime wipes out photographs of political heretics.

Though clever, she did not work at school. She would stare for hours out at the sea, as if in search of that elusive father whom she had been told about by her neighbour. Underneath the waves somewhere he was, fined down to bones, the man who had made her, the lover of her pale, doomed mother. So she would not listen to the teacher, would only attend really if he was talking about geography, but not about any other subject. And though he punished her she would not obey.

Nor did she make friends. Even in her play she had been set apart. If no slights were available she would look for some. She would fight the other girls who shouted names at her. She saw nothing beautiful in the island, but only felt pain, pain. Even the magnificent flowering of spring she did not feel in her heart and was more at home with the gauntness, the wintriness.

When there were visitors in the house she stayed in her own room and that was what her aunt wanted – for wasn't she a stigma, a mark of shame? She would strain at the keyhole to hear what they were saying about her, but she could only hear a susurrus of voices like the rustlings of leaves and could not make out the conversation. So for her there were two languages, the open one which was spoken around her and the other sniggering one which she could hardly ever distinguish.

And of course when she became a teenager there were no dances for her, oh, certainly not. How could she go to a dance? Wasn't that where her own mother had been corrupted? Weren't the voices of boys, urgent and pleading, the double voices of Satan himself? And when they spoke didn't they tell lies? Didn't they, in the interests of the flesh, make promises which would never be kept? And so on autumn nights she would lie in the house and listen to the beat of boots on the stone, and the music of the melodeon, while the moon was red in the skies and the fragrances swam about her, and her aunt knitted perpetually with pursed lips.

How lonely she was in those days; she had no friends, for even girls had the lusts of the flesh. She was like a prisoner despised for her very existence. She was given her jail food and nothing else. And only once had she broken down and wept in front of a young woman teacher who had gone to see her aunt and had been driven from the house for being no better than she should have been, since she had been at a dance when she should have been attending to her pupils and their homework.

Her mother she couldn't remember at all. Not at all. Nor of course her father, who wandered about the sea and might now be drifting outside Hong Kong or Valparaiso.

She had once written an essay in which she had said that her father was a sea captain, gruff and strong against storm and tempest, and the man teacher had glanced at her curiously before handing it back. And of course she played with the dolls her other aunt had given her (for the religious one didn't believe in dolls). These dolls were her love. She would be rescued in her little theatre by a man who came from the sea, water streaming down his beard, and she and her mother would live with him for ever. But generally she wasn't allowed to play much with her dolls.

She hated her aunt. She hated her with an inflexible hatred. Her self-righteousness appalled her. For she would never admit that she was wrong. Not even in the smallest things. For instance, if her aunt couldn't find her knitting needles she would say that Jean had deliberately hidden them, and when later she would find them fallen down inside the sofa she wouldn't apologise.

'Why, why, did you take me to live with you at all?' Jean had once shouted at her.

And her aunt had said quite calmly, looking up from her knitting, 'It was my duty of course.'

My duty, my duty, my duty. Duty was everything. There was no love, only this inflexible duty. It ruled people's lives. It made them unlovable. It made her say later to her husband, 'It's only out of a sense of duty you want your mother in Glasgow, that's all it is, if you examine it.' Duty was a terrible thing. It was death itself. It was the shadow that hung over the island.

I do not belong here, I do not belong anywhere. She hated the big mahogany wardrobes, the big mahogany sideboards; she craved lighter furniture, lightness of whatever kind. But there was no lightness. One night she woke up screaming, almost choking, clutching at her throat. She felt as if she was being strangled to death, while through the window the indifferent moon peered at her.

She would sometimes sit on a headland and gaze out at the sea, at the blue hills of the mainland seen in the distance. She would hear, carried on the breeze, the voices of the exiles, of the dead. And far below, she would watch the ducks skimming over the water and in the air distant smoke rising from ships' funnels. I must be dependent on myself, she thought.

I must meet my aunt with silence, that is my strongest weapon, and the weapon my aunt hates the most.

For the aunt believed that she was being good and kind to her, and that the fault lay in Jean, that she was showing no gratitude. Why, where would she be now if the aunt hadn't taken her in? A tramp on the streets most likely, or even dead, and yet did she thank her at any time? Not at all. Did she show respect, even? Why, not at all. What therefore was she but a recalcitrant stubborn mule? That impudent look of hers, how could anyone bear it? And why did she want to know about her father, that trash, whoever he was?

No, she had done her best for her and when the time came she would wash her hands of her – in fact, the sooner she was out of the house the better. There would be peace and stillness, not this eternal tension. Why, one night, the child in a terrible temper, had threatened that she would set the house on fire. Her sister had certainly brought a brat into the world, but what could you expect from a child conceived in sin? And even in church she sniggered, from her very earliest days, calling the minister a funny bald man. Surely there was a devil in her?

There came the day when she left the island and never went back.

But before that, let it be said that her aunt had partially accomplished her work in spite of Jean's antagonism. Let it be said that Jean did learn to believe that men were treacherous, that she was a pariah, that she had to make her own life as best she could, that her mother had been deceived by a man who floated in the water somewhere where no one could ever find him now or hold him responsible for his actions, far from courts of justice. It was a flawed girl who set off for her first job, saying a cold goodbye to her aunt, and holding her case as she stepped on to the bus, turning her inflexible face on the island and on that loveless woman who thought that she had done her duty by her. In a cold, clear voice she said, 'I shall never see you again. I shall send you money to pay for my past lodgings.' The last look she had of her aunt was her standing there in black, outlined against the wandering sea, her grey hair blowing in the wind. She bought her ticket and sat quietly at the back of the bus. She had no regrets at all about leaving. Her farewell words had been spoken to her aunt in English. Gaelic was too intimate for the distance she felt from her. She hadn't kissed her.

And later there was the business of that big mahogany wardrobe which Martin wanted as a memento of his mother. Maybe it was because he remembered her hanging his suits there when he was young, or maybe it was a sign of the solidity and security of his childhood: in any case it was a big shiny wardrobe. And Jean said, 'It's too big for this house. Can't you see that?' Though that wasn't what she meant. She really meant, Can't you see that this is my coffin coming to haunt me again? But that time at least Martin had stood out against her, had fought her to the death for that big wardrobe, so that it became symbolic of what lay between them and might rise with bitter teeth like a monster at any time. And when they were trying to manoeuvre the wardrobe into the house (the Glasgow removal men cursing and swearing so that she had to tell them to stop) she said to Martin, 'I told you so.' But they had eventually managed to get it into the house, and Martin had won, and some of the island was there, some of his mother, though it was only wood, this large mahogany cave. She wouldn't hang any of her clothes in it, it would be as if she were imprisoning herself in its darkness. Only Martin's clothes hung there, and he had to hang them there himself, placing mothballs in the darkness so that he would catch the exact tang of his childhood and be forgiven by his dead mother through furniture that had belonged to her. It was the coffin that had never gone into the earth, that stood upright, that would retain not her rotting bones but a memory of her flowery dress, which was like a meadow in spring when she was young and happy and humming about the house.

Her job in Aberdeen was as a receptionist in a hotel: she had seen the advertisement in an island paper. From the very beginning she was neither frightened nor homesick; she felt free, having a room of her own, not knowing anyone about her, booking people in by phone, handing them out their keys, these transient voyagers. The hotel itself was a large one, pretty new, with blue carpets on all the floors, long corridors off which the rooms were, and leather-seated bars with dim lighting, an almost hushed atmosphere, rather like a hospital, reminding her of that too when she saw some of the cleaners standing at lifts with their big foamy mounds of sheets.

She would sit in her room reading or listening to the radio, feeling not at all lonely, but relaxed, for no one here bothered her, there was no pressure on her, and she could do what she liked when she had finished her work. No one knew that she was illegitimate, no one directed her to church on Sunday (and she didn't go), no one insisted that she was a sinner, no one, in short, cast a black shadow over her. And so she could read the books which she had borrowed from the library (many of them about other countries, for these were the ones she liked best) or lie on her bed listening to the songs which told her of happy lovers.

Her freedom was complete. The customers continually changed so none of them could know anything about her or question her life. They were not like the people at home, fixed in their destiny, travelling the same deepening ruts day after day, in a village which never changed and would never change. There were flowers too in her room and she loved flowers.

At weekends and sometimes in the evenings she walked about the city, along roads she had never seen before. She would stop and go in for a cup of coffee, or sit in a park among roses beside a stream where fishermen were sunk to their waists, their rods flashing in the light. Immense city, how different it was from the village! There were no encounters with familiar people, all encounters were new, and standing at the corners of streets she would wonder, Which will I take now? they will both be original journeys for me.

Sometimes she would stand and watch the customers coming out of the theatre, the men in evening dress, the women in long glowing gowns, and there in the sunset they would chat to each other. She even went to plays in that very theatre, gazing with fascination at the ceilings decorated with cherubs, at the red and gold of the seats, at the mysterious curtains. When the curtains parted it was as if she was entering another country which would refresh

29

the stagnant world from which she had come with its miraculous seething imagery.

She took to visiting the art gallery and studying the paintings and in particular she liked the one by Vermeer which showed a big hefty girl pouring milk into a jar, the light playing about her. She was a peasant with big arms and elbows.

She watched the world like an outsider, a spectator, a voyeur, but one night had to walk fast through one of the old areas of the city while a drunk shouted and swayed and staggered after her. And at the market she saw some women with handbags and rouged cheeks standing insolently, hands on hips, and she knew perfectly well who they were. But her own purity was absolute.

And the fact was that for a few weeks at any rate she was perfectly happy. Using the phone she directed people to transient rooms, she passed the time of day with them as they came in with their cases; she was efficient but slightly distant, she was cool and yet polite.

The first year she saved up for a holiday in Germany; she travelled on her own by coach. She saw Cologne, she saw Munich, she saw smaller cities and towns, she admired the cleanliness, the new buildings, and she was not frightened by the fact that she did not know the language, that she could easily become lost in that forest of gutturals. No, she wasn't at all frightened, and when she came home and counted her money she sent what she had left to her aunt in payment for the 'sense of duty' that she had shown her. But she didn't even send her a postcard from Germany nor even considered it.

(One glimmering evening, though she was unaware of it, she passed her future husband, Martin, then a student in the city, who was clinking a can in the procession for Charities Day. He did not speak to her, nor she to him, but it was a little oddity that those who believed in predestination might have relished. Later of course they would talk about predestination in which neither of them believed.)

However, a girl in the hotel was watching her – the other receptionist who was from the city of Aberdeen. And one day (a fine east coast morning) she said to her, 'You don't seem to be having much fun, Jean.'

And Jean said, 'What do you mean?'

The girl, whose name was Shirley and who was a bright blonde, said to her, 'Well, you never go anywhere. You never meet any men. What do you do with yourself in that room all the time?' For Shirley couldn't believe that any girl could be happy without men.

'After all,' she continued, with a considering look which from anyone else might be thought insulting, 'you're good-looking, though your hair could be done in a more attractive way. You're also very serious and that attracts men.'

'I'm quite happy as I am, thank you,' said Jean.

'How can you be? You've been here for three months and when you go off work no one knows what you do with yourself. I'm not being nosy. I'm just trying to help.' (Which she truly was, since she couldn't understand why Jean quite voluntarily and from deliberate intent wished to be, like Greta Garbo, alone.)

And because she had a kind heart she persisted. And persisted. And persisted.

Even telling her that she was, would you believe it, going out with a young doctor whom she had met at a dance, and of whom she had hopes, not to mention ambitions . . . It was a question of patience and more patience, pretending to be a fly while you were in fact the spider. That was the essence of courtship, said the apparently worldly wise Shirley, whose temporary good looks had indeed attracted a young doctor and whose ambition was to be like one of the richer customers of the hotel, with fine leather cases, lovely clothes, a big car.

Eventually Jean gave in. She consented to take part in a foursome which would include a friend of the young doctor, a shy young man rather like herself. After all it would only be a matter of having dinner in the hotel, perhaps followed by a visit to the theatre. And would Jean let Shirley advise her on her hair and her clothes? – not that she was being impertinent but, after all, a little advice did no harm to anybody.

Thus the evening of the foursome came. At one time Jean was so terrified that she insisted on cancelling it, said she could on no account go . . . didn't know what to say, was unworthy, was not at all good-looking, what could these young men find interesting in her? And anyway she didn't drink and they wouldn't like that. She looked in the mirror and didn't like what she saw: wasn't her nose slightly too large, and as for her legs, weren't they too muscular? – even though Shirley had chosen a tight skirt for her.

But the foursome did take place. The friend whom the young doctor brought along was a psychiatrist, and this didn't please Jean (had this perhaps been deliberate on Shirley's part?) and the result was that she would hardly speak to him and defiantly, because of her nervousness, began to drink while the psychiatrist, it seemed to her, studied her.

At one crucial stage she shouted out, 'I'm illegitimate. What do you think of that?' And ran from the table and went to her room and wept, and though Shirley banged on the door insisted on waiting in there and wouldn't come out. And realising in the clear Aberdeen morning what she had done, she immediately resigned her job, looked for another one, and was on her way to Glasgow a week later.

(To meet, though she did not know it, Martin. To be brought closer and closer, though she did not know it, as she gazed through the window of the train at the North Sea and its glittering waters, to her wedding to a man whom she had seen without realising that she had done so. To be embroiled again with that island which would not let her go, with his mother, with his language, with himself. And yet throughout all that journey to recall with embarrassment, an embarrassment so intense that she squirmed in her seat, her drunken outburst at the table, the surprised expressions on the faces of her companions, as if she had deliberately broken a glass in front of them, as if she had set off a bomb in the middle of that napery, while the bottle of red wine sat tilted in its basket on the table. Leaving behind her, because of her stupidity, a city she had loved more than she had loved any other place, a city that had been good to her, had given her freedom, had somehow in its sparkling granite appealed to her innermost nature, and all for one moment of reckless revelation which had shocked her friend and her friend's friends. Leaving behind her the room that went with the job, with its radio and her books, and its flowers, and now having to find in Glasgow lodgings of some kind close to the travel agency where she would henceforth work.

What a fool she had been: but there had been no alternative, she had to leave. And she gazed out at the cold glittering North Sea, at the lighthouse, at the ships that voyaged there and she felt bereaved, with a physical longing for the gardens of Aberdeen, its roses, its granite, its theatre, its art gallery.)

And she felt it even more so when she saw Glasgow for the first time as the train pulled into Queen Street Station. Why, this was a derelict place, this was a cheap city of brick, this was a toothless ancient woman, a slattern. When she asked for the tourist office she was guided there by a small woman who came from Stirling and who talked incessantly so that Jean wondered whether she was quite all there. But she did find temporary lodgings and took a taxi to them.

The room she was guided to was in a cheap hotel. She couldn't shut the door because someone had removed the lock. There were scars on the sideboard, and she stayed awake all night while a juke box played in the bar below. She couldn't even eat her breakfast, though the waitresses were kind enough. So with her case she left that place, as if it had been a nightmare better forgotten, and sought other lodgings.

How at first she hated Glasgow! How at night she hated the yellow lights as they changed from pink and glowered over the rainy streets (for in those nights it always seemed to be raining). How she hated the ugliness, the second-rateness, how it was only that early experience of isolation that sustained her, how she felt twice-orphaned in that immense chaotic city, with its poverty and its disorder. Oh God, how could human beings live in this place, how could they endure the greyness, the rawness, the disintegration, the clocks that never showed the correct time? It was as if she had come to the very opposite of the world of her childhood which had been tightly drawn and knotted around her. While here there was a looseness, a negligence, which made her feel that she didn't exist at all. She would even touch herself to test if she was there.

One night she heard a drunk singing in Gaelic and stood for a moment half undecided as to whether she should speak to him, but then turned away, drawing her cloak of stone around her. No, no, no, not even orphaned as I am will I speak.

(And even when she got the letter saying that her aunt had died of cancer, she would not write home and only felt relief that her debt to duty was paid, for she could not send her monthly payments to the grave. No, no, I will not go to the funeral, I owe her nothing, or rather I owe her, among other things, my outburst in Aberdeen, and she tore the letter into little bits in her room in the lodging-house and threw them into the waste-paper basket which sat below the picture of the man in the Highland kilt.)

Not that her landlady came from the Highlands, she came from Dundee. She had written (in her own handwriting) a set of commandments which hung on the inside of the lodgers' bedroom doors.

ALL LODGERS MUST BE IN BY ELEVEN P.M.
LODGERS MUST CONSULT THE LANDLADY IF
    THEY REQUIRE A BATH.
PERSONAL RADIOS MUST NOT BE PLAYED TOO
    LOUD.
BREAKFAST IS BETWEEN 8 AND 9: ON SUNDAYS
    BETWEEN 8.30 AND 9.30.

She had taken a pride in drafting out the regulations, as if she were a writer, and would sometimes change them if a new infringement not covered by the original rules came to her attention. Lodgers, she knew, would try and outwit you if they could; that was what one must understand about lodgers.

She was a big fat woman who was always trailed by her small plump son. She regarded all her lodgers as enemies, as infiltrators who would scar her furniture if they could, eat more than they should and foam luxuriantly in her meagre water. So she was continually on the defensive. No, you can't get more coal, you have enough there already, and in any case do you know how much coal costs? And for some odd reason she was always forgetting to put sugar on the table. (There were a number of theories, not at all complimentary, about that.)

Apart from Jean herself the boarding-house was occupied by irreverent students, one of whom was chosen to negotiate about the coal. His triumph was to refer darkly to something that he called the Equity Board which was there to protect students and was able to close down a boarding-house if a certain standard of heating wasn't reached. It was this student who was later accused of scratching her sideboard, though in fact it was the cat that had done it.

Apart from the students, there was a man who stayed in the room above her and moved wardrobes and sideboards during the night. He said he never slept but read novels perpetually, sometimes going for long walks through the deserted streets. But she never discovered what insomnia had to do with moving furniture.

'These students never do any work,' Mrs Green

would say to her in confidence. 'There's one of them, and a law student too, who climbed in through the window of the living-room last night. Drunk, too, he was, and when I said to him, "Mr Lawrence, what do you think you're doing?" he said, "Sugar," – that's what he called me – "Sugar, have you heard me playing the guitar below your window all night? And because you would not show your dear face I thought I would climb in and see you." And he fell on the floor and puked right at my feet. He'll have to go. Look at my shoes. I can't get the puke off. There's only one of them does any work and that's the medical student, and I've my suspicions of him too ever since I found words carved into the bottom of one of the chairs in his room.'

'What words?' said Jean.

'"Sugar, I love you,"' said the landlady, blushing. 'These were the very words.'

And her husband, thin-moustached, pale-faced, and with a cleft palate, repaired and repaired his motor bike on which he used to go for long rides into the countryside. 'Stewart Moss' the students called him as, goggled, he zoomed away from the boarding-house towards the red sky to the west.

And as the sugar disappeared from the table, so also did the butter, till they reminded Mrs Green of the omission. Eventually they thought they would be confronted by an empty table as article after article was withdrawn, till Mrs Green would eventually subject them to starvation. (Later, Martin was to tell her a story of some Belgian visitors to a bed and breakfast place who had carefully wrapped in bags what they had not eaten – rolls, butter, jam, bread – and had taken it away with them.)

All this time, of course, Jean was working in the travel agency with her three girl companions and the spotty-faced Mr Smith. And she enjoyed it too. In essence it was rather like being a receptionist, for she directed people not to rooms but to countries and used the phone constantly, as she had done in her previous job. It was a busy travel agency and there was not much time for conversation, but she liked her fellow workers, who called her Jean from the very first day and not Miss Macleod as they had in the hotel.

'Say a few words of Gaelic to us,' said Irene one day to her. But she wouldn't, she refused point-blank, and it had been passed off with Joyce speaking some words of Swedish which she had learned while on holiday in Stockholm.

'Why don't you go to, what do you call them, a *ceilidh*?' said Joyce. 'I was at one once with a highland friend. There was a lot of men with kilts and bony knees.'

Jean bent over a document which she was filling in, and didn't answer.

'Lovely,' said Daphne, 'really lovely.'

'Ladies from hell, they used to call them,' said Mr Smith, and glancing at Jean turned back to his typewriter.

(I wonder what he meant by that, thought Jean, and decided that he hadn't meant anything. He was a nice man and slightly younger than her.)

'Yes, madam, of course the temperature in Austria at that time of year will not be too high . . . '

'No, no, madam, they won't arrest you in Russia if you have a camera, and they do provide you with towels . . . '

'If you would wait a moment, sir, I'll tell you the exact exchange rate . . . '

And Daphne said, 'I wish I was in Rome right now.'

I'm not ugly, thought Jean, gazing down at herself in the bath – which she had had to go through the correct procedure in order to have. I thought I was, but I am not. Perhaps my legs are not so elegant, but the rest is fine. It is my mind that bothers me the most. And she stretched out her legs in the water and immediately thought of her unknown father floating in an unknown sea, bumping against rocks, being fined down to bone, while the ocean hummed around him its salt song. And her breasts were like white rocks shining in the water, and her pubic hair was seaweed, and above her, even in the bathroom, were set Mrs Green's commandments.

'Actually,' said Iain Thomson, a student who was later to break down before his exams, 'Mrs Green was a gauleiter who managed to get out of Germany heavily disguised as a landlady. She was doing experiments on how little food prisoners can exist on and still work. Her moustache gives her away. She wanted to emigrate to Argentina, but ended up in Glasgow because she was too mean to pay the fare.'

She saw herself reflected in Brueghel's *Misanthrope*, just to the right of the Misanthrope himself with his long black cloak, his cowl and white beard, and just above the encircled youth who was robbing the old man of his purse. The Misanthrope reminded her, in his fixed, doomed gravity, of the old men and

39

women of the island from which she came. At the very back of the windmill there were some sheep and a shepherd.

'Because the world is so faithless I am going into mourning', said the inscription.

In the gallery itself there was only one other person, a young man with a moustache in a tweed jacket and flannels. She noticed in the glass of the frame that he was looking at her. She gazed more intently at the painting.

'Gloomy, isn't it?' said the young man.

She didn't answer.

'I mean the world isn't as bad as that, not in my experience, or wouldn't you agree?'

She turned away without speaking, and walked out of the room, the young man staring after her.

As her heels clicked on the pavement on her way home she didn't look back, but if she had she would have seen that he was following her. She was the Misanthrope in her green cloak walking through Glasgow.

The following day she was surprised to receive a card from him (she knew it was him because he mentioned the gallery). 'Sorry,' he wrote, 'I didn't mean to offend you. My name is Martin Macleod and I am a university lecturer. I am not in the habit of speaking to strange girls.' It was addressed to her personally at the correct address. The landlady later told her that a young man had asked who she was, saying that she had left a book behind her in the gallery. It was a copy of a book of Brueghel's paintings.

Why did she go back to the gallery? She didn't know. Was it that she was tired of her lodgings? Was it that she wished to meet him again? Was it that she did not wish to abandon her paintings because of him? She went back at the same time. He was there.

'You needn't have run away,' he said. 'I am quite harmless. I came every night on the chance that you might be here.'

She could hardly believe him.

On the other hand she didn't wish to stalk out. After all, the gallery was open to everybody. Why should she be forced away from it by this persistent young man? She was compelled into speech.

'I'm sorry,' she said, 'I don't know you and I don't wish to know you.'

'Why not?' he asked abruptly.

Hardly expecting such an answer she didn't know what to say.

'Am I a dwarf or a layabout or a delinquent that you don't wish to speak to me? Look at me. I'm presentable enough, am I not? In fact I have worn a tie for the occasion. I knew you would come back. I come here quite often and I find the paintings refreshing. You see, my study is language. And the paintings are silent.'

Having committed herself to language she found that she couldn't very well withdraw from him except by walking speechlessly about the gallery studying the paintings, or leaving the gallery altogether, which she didn't want to do.

'There's no harm in talking to you, is there?' he said. 'I am not trying to drive you out of the gallery or anything like that.'

She listened for the first time, not just to what he was saying but to the accent as well. It was the accent of her own island. She was perplexed and horrified. Here was the island again pursuing her, even into the

41

centre of art itself. She shuddered as if a shadow had passed over her.

'I . . . ' she began.

'Look,' said Martin, 'why don't you come with me for a coffee? There is a restaurant attached to the gallery. If you like, I won't speak to you at all. It's tiring walking around the gallery. I'm not liable to attack you. I can bring you references if you like from my head of department who knows Icelandic.'

His serious expression when he spoke this nonsense made her smile. Was this the devilish situation of which her aunt had warned her? In this room with its many lovely paintings, was this the first manipulation of Satan? No, she had better leave immediately. But if she left now what would she do but read or knit in her room, which wasn't all that warm, or listen to the radio in the lounge while the students studied half-heartedly? She made for the door. He danced in front of her. She stopped.

'I swear,' he said. 'It will only be for a coffee. You can pay for it yourself if it will make you happier.'

And he smiled again. That moustache, that brig-and-like moustache. Was that not a warning of devilry?

I must go, she thought, and then, Why should I go? My life is in my own power. And she went with him for a coffee. And yes, she was tired, and glad of the chair.

'Let me introduce myself,' said Martin. 'My name is Martin Macleod and I am a lecturer in the Celtic Department of the university. I can show you my driving licence if you like and I also have an Access card and a cheque card.' He fumbled in his pockets. She smiled again.

She drank her coffee quietly. And having drunk her coffee she was committed to speech.

'How did you find out my name?'

'I followed you. I walked behind you all the way to your digs. I would have taken a taxi if you had walked further than you did.'

'Why did you do that?'

'I wanted to see you again. You looked very like the Misanthrope in the painting. I wondered whether after all you were.'

She smiled again.

'Your landlady was rather surprised. She doesn't strike me as being a fan of Brueghel. At first she wouldn't tell me your name. Then I gave her a pound and she did tell me.'

'You come from Raws?'

'Yes, I do. I was born there. I am now living in Glasgow digs just like yourself. By the way is there something about me that you don't like? Do I have BO, for instance? Whenever you see me you head for the door.'

'No, it's not that. It's just . . . '

'Just what?'

'Oh, nothing. You are very persistent.'

'Yes, I am. Where do you come from?'

'From Raws,' she said.

'Now isn't that amazing? You might almost say it was predestination. I must tell you about my uncle some time and how he met his wife.'

She quickly put on her gloves and said, 'I must be going.'

'Can I see you again?' said Martin, standing up.

In a flurry, she said, 'I don't— '

'Look,' he said. 'There's a film on tomorrow night. Do you want to come? You don't need to say now. Here is my phone number. Phone between three and seven. Any time between these hours. I'll be home then.'

'Three,' she said. 'And seven.'

'Yes,' he said. 'That's the privilege of being a lecturer.'

She put the card with the phone number in her pocket and left the gallery. In a strange way it was as if the street itself appeared more friendly.

To speak, to be forced to speak, if someone speaks to you. She hadn't really wanted to speak to him, but had been compelled to do so. And by taking his coffee had been impelled along the road of further speech. Should she not stop now? Did she want to go on? She stared at her meagre room, at the flowery wallpaper, at the wash-basin, slightly cracked, at the mirror with the foliage round it, at the blank chest of drawers. This was not her room; she had never really had a room that she could call her own, one she could furnish and decorate herself. And the meagreness of the days, the rising in the morning on one's own, the setting off towards the office to work on her own behalf, that was the routine of the days. True, the students amused her in their expeditions and plans for coal and sugar, but nevertheless she was on her own, wasn't she? Who did she speak to? To the girls in the office, now and again to the landlady, sometimes to the students, but who did she really speak to? Was it not time to think of that? Was it not time for her to speak . . . to tell . . . to narrate . . . who she was, who she thought she was, who she might be? To reveal . . .

And so she did after all ring Martin, and so they

44

went to the pictures. And she learned to speak. And the story changed.

But she would not speak Gaelic to him, ever.

Their courtship was not an easy one, quite the contrary, so that sometimes Jean would ask herself, Is this love, or is it a protection from loneliness, from my landlady's flowery wall?

Thus, *item*, they had quarrels about intellect. 'You are looking down on me because you are a lecturer,' she would say. And Martin would look at her in genuine astonishment. Why, rather, he thought of her as bright. 'But, no,' she insisted, 'the frivolous things you say, you don't take life seriously when you are with me. You referred to some Gaelic woman writer as having a 'pro's' style. What did you mean by that?' For she actually thought of her mother in connection with his statement, while he was making a flashing remark which he thought quite amusing. No, of course he wasn't referring to her mother, he said, he didn't even know her or anything about her.

And, *item*, why did he object to her being sometimes late for their dates? Did he not know that it was a problem to have a bath in her digs where there were so many students, and also a landlady who was all-seeing, altogether contemptible? Did he not know that in digs it wasn't easy for a girl to prepare herself for going out, especially when she wished to look her best, and most especially if they were going out to dinner? It was easy enough for him, all he had to do was put on his suit, which incidentally was not as well pressed as it should be, did he know that, with his airy-fairy jokes? And also did he shave as closely as he ought? She didn't think he did. Why, he said,

45

he never thought about clothes, no one remarked on them. Naturally not, she replied. Did he think they would, were they likely to do so? But they might think so just the same.

And, of course, clothes were important to her as they were to any woman. Why, she could dress as well as anyone else, she would have him know. And had he not found out whether the other women were going to be wearing long dresses at the party they were going to? Otherwise she might appear a total fool.

Then, *item*, why had he spent such a long time talking to Miss Hope who, she knew, was in his department, but nevertheless . . . ? She hadn't known anyone and therefore she had to sit on her own, while he laughed and smiled and drank and made his silly jokes, and forgot all about her. (That particular quarrel had to be solved by means of a large bouquet of flowers delivered to her digs late at night and carried to her room by a disapproving landlady.)

So that sometimes she would go out with him and sometimes not, and in the office listened to the history of other romances but didn't refer to her own at all.

She grew fonder and fonder of Glasgow: how could she ever have anticipated she would like it so much? She, the orphan of the city. She no longer thought of Aberdeen at all. Glasgow itself was like an orphan badly treated, humiliated, foggily growing into its own clarity, yet still resilient after rape, robbery, sustained attack and assault, whereas Aberdeen was like a girl who belongs to the upper classes, rides a horse in green through quiet streets, is set in aristocratic profile against granite.

'*Item*,' she would say. 'What did you see in me?'

And Martin would answer, 'It was like this. I saw you looking at that *Misanthrope* painting, that tall death-like figure in black, and you were wearing a green cape, and I wondered what you were thinking. You looked so young, so unprotected, and my heart turned over. And there was sadness there too, as if you were not looking at a painting at all but rather into a mirror. And then you turned away, and you looked so imperious . . . And so I followed you through the streets of Glasgow winking and blinking its contemporary language.'

'*Item*, why did I go out with you? It was because . . . because . . . I can't confess to you. It was because of that hateful becalmed Victorian room.' And Martin laughed as if a victory over wallpaper was sufficient for him. And in the cinema as he put his arm around her so that her head rested on his shoulder it was as if he was sheltering her from the storms of the world.

For he himself had had a happy childhood. He remembered it quite clearly – fishing for trout, chasing small eels in rivers, following his father at the plough in a cloud of seagulls, making little paper boats which he sailed on ponds, going to football matches in astoundingly red sunsets. Oh, his childhood had been a happy one. And his adolescence successful and also happy (like the time the Celtic Society had gone for a picnic and they had filled the boot of the bus with drink and had a piper playing all the way to the rustic spot they had chosen, and played just one game of rounders and then drank steadily for the rest of the day till they arrived back in the city plastered, the piper staggering up and down the aisle of the bus with bubbles of beer coming out of his chanter).

So he couldn't really understand her childhood and adolescence.

And, *item*, she wasn't interested in children. He had thought when they got married that she would change, but she didn't. She didn't want children at any price, she shouted angrily. So he had comforted her sometimes in the middle of the night as she would cry for no reason, as she would wake out of nightmares with black men with black wings pursuing her, as she would find herself weeping in stony deserts, as sometimes she would sit up in bed unable to speak, gagging on her words. These nights frightened him, almost destroyed him. And he had to walk carefully, as if he were bearing a trayful of glasses across a minefield.

But when she was in a good humour how he loved her. Why, her spontaneity was so life-enhancing. She would suddenly dance in the middle of the living-room if a dancing programme came on the television, or she would dress up in wigs, masks, odd clothes, and they would horseplay raucously like two demented people. She was often dressing up in those early days in long gowns, short jackets, eastern skirts, gipsy blouses, as if she wished to be different each day, each hour, like water.

In those happiest days of her life she scoured the city for exactly the kind of clock she wanted, for exactly the wood for the bookcases which towered from floor to ceiling. She even bought Martin a beautiful desk with lots of drawers and an old-fashioned inkstand on the top with a quill stuck in it. She had perfect pitch in her taste; it was unlearned instinct, the difference between those who learn a language late in life and those who have it from the beginning. He was continually astonished by it, for he himself did not care for possessions, for appearances.

And one day she created the most bitter scene

over a vase he had accidentally broken. 'That vase was mine,' she shouted in a childish rage. 'I bought it with my own money.' (It had a picture of a Greek seascape on it, beautiful enough in itself but not spectacularly so, Martin thought.) But it was as if she had lost the whole earth. He couldn't sustain her raging onslaught and had to leave the house and walk up and down for what seemed to be hours. And when he came back she told him she had almost rung the police, thinking something had happened to him. Her insecurity was awesome, beyond belief. That vase had almost become part of her; it wasn't really greed in any ordinary sense, the vase was like a raft which she clutched in a tempestuous sea.

And the times he tried to speak to her in Gaelic were best forgotten . . . It was as if he had appointed himself her guardian, without whom she would otherwise die. And yet he loved her, of course he loved her, for behind the outer writing she showed there was another faint writing which he could glimpse now and again and which he wished to draw into the sunlight like fading ink. If his love was great enough . . .

Oh, she tested him, she tested him to the limit (and perhaps in his early negligence he tested her to the limit too). For he was a careless maker of mots, there was something of the perpetual student in him. He would say, when watching a film about an African tribe singing, 'Where is the mod★ next year?' and burst into ludicrous laughter. While her sense of humour was not as piercing, as delicate, as his. He saw the world as phantasmal, ironic, he didn't have enough 'bottom'. And that was why he would never

★A highland literary and musical festival.

become a professor. For to become a professor it was necessary to view the world in a certain way, which he couldn't train himself to do. Though in certain areas he was deadly serious; in the matter of language, for example.

But this sense of honour was so perpetually present to him that he saw the world as theatre (at least in his early days) and perhaps that was why he liked her when she dressed up and so many different selves peeped out from behind her long gowns.

One might think that they would not have been happy together, but they were in a deep sense, perfectly happy. The only thing that threatened them was her moods, which might not appear for long periods, but suddenly – perhaps when they were drinking a glass of wine together – emerge as frighteningly puritanical, frighteningly severe, so that for days afterwards she would wear her hair drawn tight in a bun, making her look fifty years old. And then the spontaneity would take over again, and she would dance her abandoned dances in the living-room. It certainly wasn't boring to be living with her, that at least could be said.

(And he would elaborate on this imagined tribe of people who would only speak about mods. There would be sixteen people in a row and one would say to another, 'I think Meg MacDucket was the best gold medallist there was.' And another would think for a while and say, 'I think, to be perfectly truthful, that Margaret MacStoochar was the best medallist. Meg MacDucket couldn't compare with her for timbre.' And he would go off into fits of laughter over the word 'timbre', for he thought it an essentially funny word. And he would maintain this fiction for a long time, one person after another defending his/her own

50

gold medallist: ending up in hysterics while she would sew or knit gravely in the powerful electric light which she had covered with a green shade, for green was her favourite colour.)

She also believed in astrology. Though he pointed out to her the difference between astrological forecasts in various papers, some even contradicting each other, she still believed in the influence of the stars shining above her, picking her out from the crowd, holding her as if in a spotlight, following her.

Their wedding had been in a registry office since she had no relations whom she wished invited, and her side of the aisle in a church would be empty. The night before the wedding they had a big quarrel in the hotel they were staying in because she insisted on sending back the food that they had been given on the grounds that it was inadequately cooked. Martin had been embarrassed, but the waiter did not seem to be at all angry. 'I've worked in hotels, I know what you can do and what you can't,' said Jean.

So they had settled down, she returning to her job at the travel agency, he fixed in his at the Celtic Department: she sending customers into the future sparkling with new experiences; he digging away at his philological roots, analysing, comparing, finding analogies, derivations, grammars.

Operatic Glasgow was all around them in its greens and blues, he seeing it through poetry as the city to which the Highlanders had emigrated, writing their songs of exile as soon as they were off the train, entering factories to learn the new permutations of time (they who had stared out at a landscape which changed only according to the seasons), some drunk, some sober, some longing for the annual holiday so that they could return to their dreams again, to the island which they had left and which waited, as they hoped, unchangingly for them.

He learned about her upbringing and was horrified. For the island had two faces, the religious one and the communal one. The religious one was communal also; it frowned on those who did not enter its rigid churches, it cast them out into outer darkness, it walked with them till they saw the right way. And on the other side there was the truly communal face smiling, pleasant, familiar. She had known one face, he the other – two distinct profiles on a coin. It was like one of those trick pictures where, if you look casually, you see a vase, but then if you scrutinise it more closely you see a face.

But her own father was drifting among the salt water, not standing or sitting four-square in a church wearing a black hat and a black coat, respectable, fixed. He wandered the alien incorruptible sea.

She wanted to travel, he didn't. He was quite happy to sit where he was: travel did not in his opinion improve one's mind – it was superficial, glancing, without depth. She, on the other hand, longed to travel: she wanted to be away from wherever she was. So they went to France, Austria, Italy, Greece. She loved the heat, he didn't. She loved the continual movement, he didn't. All that he brought back with him were linguistic comparisons: a word in French which looked like a Gaelic word like *église* and *eaglais*. She would try out her fragments of French or German unblushingly; he was much more circumspect. Surprisingly, she hated the cathedrals – the candles, the incense, the apparatus of Catholicism: he, on the other hand, found them beautiful, aesthetic, lovable.

The question of language obsessed him. Crossing into another language was like crossing barbed wire, languages fought each other to the death like animals. Some survived, some did not. Some of them were at the centre of their time, some were not – Gaelic wasn't. It was off to the edge: imperialistic English was calmly devouring it, like a lion sleepily devouring a deer. It was the orphan, the Cinderella among the sophisticates.

One grew up inside the perimeter of a language, it defined the way one saw the world. He had read somewhere that the reason the Eastern countries had not developed so fast as the Western in scientific matters was connected with language. The Western countries had grammars which consisted of subject, predicate, object; that is, they were an active linguistic aggrandisement. And what Western science did was to subject the world to its dominance, mirroring the language in that way. Western science manipulated nature because this was what its language taught it to do. Eastern, for instance Indian, grammar wasn't grasping, imperialistic. So it was bound not to develop so fast in scientific terms, for it did not wish to change nature to its own desires.

He studied language in its wider connotations. He read Wittgenstein and those of his disciples who believed that philosophy was simply a matter of asking the right question, of using the right words like keys to unlock doors. He couldn't discuss this with Jean, not because she wasn't bright but because she wasn't interested. Why should she be? She had her own interests. She collected vases, usually with pictures painted on them like seascapes or classical legends. She would scour the shops for them. They were fragile, beautiful, sometimes local. They flashed with colour, reflected light from each other, were timeless, ardent, brilliant. Yet their fragility was never in doubt.

Once he had come upon her unexpectedly staring at a vase which had a picture of Orpheus and Eurydice on it. Eurydice was disappearing with a flicker of cloak, Orpheus was clutching his lyre tightly in his hand, his gaze half towards her, half towards the lyre. She was a ghost vanishing into the dark, and yet he was immersed in his music. Yet what was it that made Martin think of the lyre as of the same wood as coffins in the island? What was it about Eurydice that broke his heart as he saw her on the edge of vanishing, as he saw Jean watching her vanishing, so that when she looked up and saw him his eyes were dim with tears, and he clutched her as if the two of them were drowning in that vase, austere and flowerless? Eurydice's gaze was fixed directly on Orpheus. She did not even plead with him, perhaps she knew him too well; all she did was reveal herself fading into the perfection of nothingness, of his art, of his new art. It was almost as if one could hear the new music rising from the lyre, the strings of life itself which were so closely connected with death.

This incident happened after he had begun to feel troubled. The trouble had come on slowly and insidiously. It was a question of being ill at ease in his life, of being continually faced with contradictions. He and Jean never talked in Gaelic and yet he was supposed to be concerned with its survival, its history, its genealogy.

And again he was in the middle of the city, in a study, in a lecture room, far from his own people, researching while his language was dying as his mother had died.

All the signals from the islands were of alarm. The children were not speaking Gaelic; they were ashamed of their own language. (Was he ashamed of it? Deep down was he ashamed of it, as of failure, as of an invalid dying behind white curtains? Why then did he not insist that Jean speak it? And where were the children that the two of them could contribute to the 'cause'?)

His life was not right.

Sometimes he would stand in front of the mirror in the mornings and question his reflection. Who are you? he would ask, and the reflection, slightly puzzled, would project back at him an enigma that he could not fathom.

He was at the wrong angle to the world. He existed in bad faith. He was unsettled, forty years old, and depressed. If he didn't watch out he would take to drink . . . like Morrison.

Like John Morrison, who sometimes dropped in on the two of them at three o'clock in the morning, whom Jean intensely disliked because he tried to paw her in the kitchen whither he would follow her for cups of black coffee; John Morrison, who never had any money and for whom Martin had to buy bottles of whisky; the brilliant John Morrison, who insulted him even as he drank his drink; the island cosmopolitan who had inherited the worst of the city and retained the worst of the island.

And, *item*, laughing, he would say to Martin, as soon as he entered, 'I see you're wearing your clan tie. This is the one you always wear when I call. Hello, Jean, still my true lover, eh?' And he laughed his sarcastic laugh.

'Listen, Martin, I have this theory,' he said, as soon as he came in. 'I think that modern Gaelic poetry is different from older Gaelic poetry in this fundamentally ... I don't suppose you have a jar handy? If you've had a visit from the Free Church minister, I suppose you will have. Thanks, old pal ... Anyway, Martin, my theory is this. The old Gaelic poetry was oral, modern Gaelic poetry is not, it is meant for the reader in his study.' (From this point onwards he completely ignored Jean, who went away into the kitchen leaving the two of them alone. Jean resented this, as if Morrison thought that she couldn't follow anything he was saying.)

'What this means, essentially,' he continued, his eyes shining, 'is that you have, among other things, the concept of irony carried to its conclusion. Irony is what a reader can appreciate in his study, not so much in oral performance. In other words, modern Gaelic poetry is approaching the condition of other modern poetry and is taking its place in the mainstream ... Is this Teacher's whisky you have here? You never had a good taste in the water of life, Martin.

'Now listen carefully, what does this mean? It means that the music which traditional Gaelic poetry had, has been eliminated. OK? This music arose from metre, assonance, etc. But if you study modern Gaelic poetry you don't find it to the same extent. And, another thing, modern Gaelic poetry has been to a great extent produced by intellectuals. What does this imply? It implies that their concerns are intellectual concerns.'

'I don't agree with you,' said Martin. 'I don't agree with you at all.'

'Oh,' and Morrison leaned back in his chair, his tiny moustache visibly trembling like an aerial, a smile on his lips.

'Not at all,' said Martin stubbornly. 'The change of style was necessary. The movement away from the

56

oral was necessary too. Society itself has changed as far as the islands are concerned and the oral is no longer so important. If you say these poets are intellectuals then why should they not be intellectual? You are falling into the trap that many people fall into, that the islanders are not interested in the intellectual, that they have no right to pronounce on the problems of the present.'

'Hey, hey,' said Morrison. 'Not at all. Wait a minute. I didn't say that. What I did say was, can we afford to lose the qualities of music that the language had in traditional poetry and replace it by a verse which is not musical? I am asking, is the loss too great? Would the loss be greater than I could bear if you were to remove that tie and I saw you as you really are? Do you remember that poem by Yeats about the yellow hair?' And he smiled his demonic malignant smile.

Martin, as usual, was put off by these gossipy interpolations but continued doggedly, 'You know perfectly well that the only way Gaelic poetry can survive is by changing. That is a law which applies to more than poetry.'

'Like the Christian faith in relation to science,' said Morrison, carefully pouring out another glass of whisky for himself.

'If you like. There is no reason why Gaelic poetry should remain within a laager.' (Here the intentional pun made Morrison salute him ironically.) 'There is no reason why it shouldn't go out into the world, express an opinion, on Vietnam if you like, on anything. In fact you could argue that Gaelic poetry was greatest when it broke free from too local concerns. You know perfectly well that much of Gaelic poetry has been occasional. There is no reason why fully articulated artistic tradition cannot be created.'

'But maybe at what expense?' said Morrison, waving his glass. 'Maybe at what expense? Listen, our problem is that the urban is not our natural habitat and urban poetry tends to be ironical, sophisticated, intellectual. You and I are examples of the urban expatriate. We read Baudelaire, if you like, but how many of the islanders do? That is why there is a gap between this poetry and the islanders. You know that.'

'What nonsense,' said Martin, who himself had taken another glass of whisky. 'What utter nonsense. There is a gap between the English poet and the ordinary person, if you like. That is nothing new. And I don't agree with you about modern Gaelic poetry. It has not divorced itself entirely from traditional Gaelic poetry. It is a half-way house. Its practitioners have kept a continuous line of development. And its concerns are not necessarily urban either. They don't have to be.'

'Yes, but who is it speaking to?' said Morrison. 'Tell me, is it speaking only to us? And if it is speaking only to us, is it any use? Its ironical echoes from Freud, who is picking them up? I can see a little man from the islands with his crystal set trying to get the wavelength. Eh, Martin? Don't you agree with me?'

'Well, then, why don't you go back and teach them about Freud?' said Martin, who was worried about Jean sitting in her kitchen alone. Martin never worried about his womenfolk, he acted as if he were a bachelor.

'Me? Why should I go back? Of course I can't go back. What could I live on there? Where would I get a job? And life there is so narrow and who could I talk to? I'm used to good talk, and where would I find it there? Would I meet someone urban, sophisticated, like yourself there?' And he smiled his wolfish grin.

(Which Martin hated, since though he had a good mind he didn't have that ability to take time off from argument, as it were, and put the dirk in casually. It was a technique that Morrison had learned from the islands themselves.)

'Listen,' said Morrison, 'when I go back I feel constricted. I know you are an idealist, but that is the way I feel. I think I'm slowly being strangled to death. Anyway, what's happened to Jean?'

'She's . . . I don't know . . . she's doing something, maybe making coffee.'

'Jean would tell us,' said Morrison with his wolfish smile. 'She's the ordinary woman . . . the one whom genius has not touched as it has touched us, eh?'

(Why do I feel compelled to argue with him? thought Martin. Why won't I throw the bad-mannered bugger out? Is it the gentle part of me that is deeply Highland that prevents me from doing so? If I really believed in what I thought, should I not throw him out? But I have to live with him in the department, that is the important thing. What is he but a tramp – an intellectual tramp, but a tramp nevertheless?)

'Tell me,' said Morrison, 'what the modern poet has produced compared with this.' And he quoted,

> Thig trì nithean gun iarraidh . . .
>
> (Three things come without seeking,
> jealousy, terror and love . . .)

'Tell me that, Martin. I rest my case,' and he laughed his Mephisthophelean laugh. At which point Jean came in.

'Ah, here she is, just at the right moment,' said Morrison, laughing. 'Three things come without seeking, jealousy, terror and love.' And he rose and linked arms with Jean. 'There you are, Martin, the triad, the great immortal triad, jealousy, terror and love.

'And how are you, Jean?'

'I'm fine.'

'Look at the way she answers. I'm fine. What a welcome! What beaded bubbles winking at the brim. I was just saying to Martin here that you are the ordinary person and, Lord, let me not be misunderstood, I love the ordinary person, what would I not give to be close to the ordinary person.' And here he clasped her tightly, while she glared at Martin. 'The ordinary person, do you remember what Chesterton said? That all his days he had been trying to ascend towards the ordinary person.'

'Which is a pose,' said Martin sharply, drinking more whisky. 'Which is a ludicrous pose.'

'Oh, you think it is a pose that I clasp my beloved Jean here and that I reverence her for being the ordinary person. You are very wrong, Martin, very wrong indeed. I see you are still an élitist.'

'Crap,' said Martin angrily, 'unmitigated crap. If there is an élitist here it is you. Why the hell don't you take a good look at yourself? A disoriented tramp, that's all you are; you don't know whether you're coming or going, you don't know where you are.'

'Temper, temper! I am quite happy here with Jean beside me. Aren't you? Is this what this outburst is about?'

'What are you talking about?' said Martin.

'Anyone would think,' said Morrison equably to

Jean, 'that Martin here didn't like me. But this is our condition of survival, isn't it, Martin? Really?'

'Your condition of survival, not mine.'

'Well, if that is the case why don't you go back to your island then? Why don't you go back to the long sunsets, the old men with beards wiser than Solomon, why don't you go back?

'What do you think, my darling?' he said, tightening his arm around Jean.

'Never,' said Jean. 'I would never go back.'

'And why not, pray?'

'I have my reasons. And now would you like a cup of coffee?'

'Nothing I would like better.' And he looked calculatingly from one to the other.

(What does his wife think of this? thought Martin. What does she think of his drinking steadily every night, invading people's houses, never coming home till four in the morning, this trampish insomniac? Ah, but he is brilliant, she might say. On the contrary, thought Martin, his brilliance is a myth like so much about the islands. His brilliance is fragile, demented, without substance. He is a man searching the midnight streets for himself, casting a long staggering shadow, exaggerated in his responses, addicted only to the mind, inhuman . . .)

'And there is your husband,' Morrison was saying to Jean while still clutching her with his left arm, his right holding the whisky glass. 'In the days when I really knew him, when we were young together, digging Celtic roots, he could be scathing and cutting. Now what is he but a middle-aged rancorous man still wearing his patriotic tie? What is this but the Gaelic menopause? I know this, you know this, but he doesn't know it. The Gaelic menopause affects men

61

strangely, it is like senile dementia, it takes them back to their childhood, so that their childhood appears more clearly to them than contemporary things. It does not cast a cold eye, on the contrary it casts a warm eye. Tell me, what do you think, Jean? You are like me, aren't you, you love the city, and there is Martin dreaming of the past as much as any of those who attend our respected mods. Isn't that right, Martin?'

'Shut up, you shit, why don't you pay for your own drink?' shouted Martin. 'Isn't it time you did so? You make me ashamed of being Highland.'

'And there you hear,' said Morrison mildly, 'the voice of the ethical man, the voice that pronounces judgement, which I am sure Jean will recognise.'

(Jean had once told him about her early circumstances and it was typical of him that he should use his knowledge of them in his argument.)

'Get the hell out of here,' shouted Martin. 'Get out. Scrounge somewhere else.'

And his attitude was so threatening that Morrison picked up his hat and left, for he was not quite drunk enough to want a fight. But Martin knew that he would act towards him in the morning as if nothing had happened.

And is it indeed the Gaelic menopause? thought Martin miserably, among the glasses which Jean cleared away in a cold silence. Was that all it was? Was he simply tired of teaching Old Irish, was he simply tired of being himself, did he wish to strike out again, to begin anew, was that all this was about? He walked over to the window and pulled the heavy velvet curtains aside. The traffic passed and passed remorselessly. Was this then the true centre of things – the city – was this the true reality, was he retreating towards a lesser reality? He could hear the clink of the glasses as Jean cleaned them in the sink. Viciously he shut the curtains again and tiptoed quietly up to Jean. He put his arms around her, but she pushed them savagely away. The bare light of the kitchen shone indifferently down on them.

'Bugger it all,' said Martin, 'bugger it all,' and then in the living-room stretched his arms out ironically, 'I am faced with the tragic choice . . . '

They fought each other. 'I'll tell you what it is,' Martin would say. 'Do you know why you took a job in the travel agency? It was so that you could avoid the island. You dream of foreign countries you would want to settle in. And there, at the back of everything, is the island.'

'And why did you bury yourself in Old Welsh and Old Irish? Was it not so that you wouldn't have to face reality? The reality of Glasgow. The reality of yourself.'

'And what is the reality of myself?'

'That you're more interested in scholarship than you are in human beings. What are you hiding from?'

Hiding from? He wasn't hiding from anything, was he? He remembered the first time he had arrived in Aberdeen, those many years ago, the terror of it, the fear of the city. Lying in his bed late at night and hearing a late singer passing below his window singing, of all things, a Gaelic song. The landlady and her old father who studied him through his thin, rimless glasses. The world which was unaware of him as he passed through it.

But that was all over now, surely? He was not frightened of Glasgow now, not at all. It was simply that it was not his home – and that was a different thing altogether. To walk through Glasgow was – how could he explain it? – to feel overwhelmed by time, by ennui, on occasion by insignificance. And was he therefore trying to make himself significant again by making the large gesture, by throwing away his lectureship and descending the ladder in search of an ideal? Was that what all this was about?

On the other hand, if she loved him would she not go back with him? For his shame was not that he had despised his language, his shame was that he had neglected it. Perhaps she was right enough, perhaps he had retreated into the world of scholarship in order to evade the real issue. It was as if his mother was dying again on the island, untended, alone.

Jean was jealous of the island, much as a lover is jealous of a rival. The island to her was a woman, it was a symbol of something that had gone wrong with their marriage. That was the way women thought, Martin was sure of it. They could be jealous of a house, a book, a friendship.

He could not go on as he was doing. He had simply lost interest. Language for its own sake was inadequate. Language was people, people were language. Language was a social thing. The difficulty was now he was thinking of leaving his scholarship, she didn't want him to.

And then it struck him right in the middle of that room. What was wrong between himself and Jean was an affair of language as well. They spoke to each other, but in a sense they were speaking across each other. He hadn't found the right question for her, nor perhaps would she listen to the question. She was answering questions which she herself had put, not the ones he had. The right question was like the island that stood bleak and tall in the middle of a wandering sea. Perhaps we were doomed never to recognise the right question when it was put to us. He imagined her as an orphan of the brine, always searching for her father, not to be found in the island, not even to be found in Glasgow.

'Listen,' he said, 'you didn't want my mother here. I know that and I understand it, but what about your own mother? Do you ever think of her? Do you never want to see the place where she was buried?' (For the islander the burial place was of the greatest importance. The body could only be happy under a certain grass, near a certain road, by a certain sea.)

'No,' said Jean, 'I don't. What would be the point?'

'Well, she must have suffered too. I know you suffered, but she must have suffered too. Can you never forgive her, and, if you can't, aren't you being like the church itself?'

'I don't remember her. It's not that I don't forgive her.'

'But you are allowing those others whom you can't forgive to separate you from her.'

'I am not separated from her. I think of her often.'

'I'm sorry,' said Martin. 'I didn't mean to bring that up. But it strikes me that it goes to the root of things, if you see what I mean.'

(To the root of things. Like when once in the garden he had tried to tug a rose out of the ground and its toughness was beyond belief. It extended for so long under the earth, under the path; and he had pulled and pulled and hacked and hacked till finally he had landed upside down among the brambles, looking up into the clear blue. How these moments sometimes came back to him with a pristine clearness, like the transparencies he had once had on his wrist, like the cigarette cards he had once collected showing football players, flowers, animals.)

'I do see,' said Jean. 'I do see,' in that voice which meant, There is some other woman, I can tell.

'I can't go back,' she said. 'I can't. Can't you see that?' How could he feel the band that tightened around her very breasts when she thought about it? Whereas for him the island was a tall sky opening above him.

But he was thinking, Can one deny one's childhood and be a whole human being? Can one? Is it possible? Was it not his duty to set her free from that prison?

'I'd like a drink,' said Jean suddenly.

Surprised, he said, 'Well, why don't you take one? A sherry, is it?'

'No,' she said, 'whisky. Whisky,' she said defiantly.

'All right, then, we'll both have one,' he said.

He recalled a night on the island when he had found a drunk man among the perfumes of flowers at the roadside, and out of the cloud of scent the man had swayingly said, 'Sauchiehall Street. I remember it. Sauchiehall Street.' And then had slumped back into the fragrant bushes again.

To teach again in his old school, was that what he wished to do? He remembered with affection Mr Trill, energetic, obsessed with Virgil and Ovid; the Bunsen Burner who was always making mistakes in his experiments; the squat, bow-legged Miss Curran; his Gaelic teacher addicted to sudden furies. Was that what he wished to do, to return to these days of sunlight and exploration? The sleepy rooms, the conversations, the girls bursting like crocuses from winter, the walks by the harbour. Was this then what he wished? To return to the scenes of his former victories? No, no, he simply wished to be more useful than he was. He wished to return to a rawer reality. He wished to make a significant sacrifice, to justify himself, to justify his life.

Jean, who was usually so silent, told the girls at the office what was happening.

Daphne was indignant. 'The bugger,' she said. 'But that's men all over. Before I divorced Bill I walked straight into the pub where he was drinking with his pals and I sat down at the table and I said, "I'd like a large vodka." And do you know what he had the impudence to say to me? "I thought you were at home with the child. You don't tell me that you left him in the house alone?" "You go back then and look after him, but I'm having my vodka," I said. And he didn't know where to look. The other men were embarrassed. That's men for you.'

Irene took a different view. She was pale-faced, bloodless, Catholic and came from a large family.

'I think', she said, 'that you should follow your husband wherever he goes. I think it's your duty.'

The other two were hilariously critical.

'Follow him wherever he goes,' said Joyce. 'He might go to hell. Are you going to follow him there? I'm with Daphne on this. It's cruelty, that's what it is. Jean here is frightened. Anyone can see that. And she loves her husband. Anyone can see that too. If I was you I'd make him jealous. I'd make him think twice about you. He's taking you for granted, that's what it is.'

'I can't say that he hasn't been good to me,'

said Jean, 'but what am I going to do if he goes back to the island and I don't go with him? I'll be back in lodgings again and I don't want that.' And she shuddered as she thought of the Victorian wallpaper, the flowery dells of her landlady's house with its smell of Mansion Polish.

'You could always get a flat,' said Daphne. 'For that matter you could move in with me.'

'Could I?' said Jean.

'I don't see why not. It's a reasonable enough place on Great Western Road. You've never been; you should visit me some time. Don't let your husband think that he's got all the cards, that's the answer. Bill outwitted me along the line. I never got a penny from the bastard.'

'But you don't understand,' said Irene, who was the most beautiful of the three of them, slim, tall, fair-haired. 'She loves her husband very much.'

'Love,' said Daphne contemptuously. 'When it comes to the point what's that? Funny thing is,' she added meditatively, 'when I see Bill now I don't feel anything for him at all. And yet at one time we were so passionate. It wasn't sex that separated us, I can tell you that. But now when I see him he's just like anyone else.'

Joyce looked up from her typewriter. 'Your husband must be mad going back to that island anyway. I was on holiday there once. It peed with rain all the time. Nothing but old shepherds and stones. And we couldn't watch the TV on a Sunday or find a café open. What does he see in that God-forsaken hole?'

'You come and see my flat some time,' said Daphne. 'Some night. I'll fix it up. Let him know you're not an orphan of the storm.' Jean's case only proved to her what she had always known, that men

68

were a shower of bastards, that they would do you all along the line if they could get away with it, that all they wanted was the one thing, to hell with everybody else, I'm all right, Jack.

When she came back at night it was as if to a disappearing house, and she felt panicky, as if a great hole was opening in her life. She didn't like Martin for confronting her with this choice of all choices. She didn't want to speak to him. And he was drinking more than he used to, that was quite clear to her. Like so many of the other islanders, she thought contemptuously: drink and religion, that is all they are fit for.

She began to think of him as if he were her aunt constricting her, returning her to the coffin of that island. She made remarks about the wardrobe.

'That ugly old thing,' she would say.

And he would say, 'It's the only piece of furniture in the house that belongs to me.'

'You can take the whole lot if you want,' she said vindictively. 'I'm not bothered. I was never worried about possessions.' (And that was true.) But she needed them as an anchor.

'If you go I've got a place to go to,' she said.

'Where?'

'I can move in with Daphne. She works with me. You've probably heard me talking about her, though you never normally listen.'

In a way he had already made up his mind. In a short while he might even hand in his resignation. He had made some enquiries about a teaching job in the school.

Sometimes she felt that this was nothing to do with language at all. It was a battle between the two of them. Which of them could stand loneliness more? Perhaps she could. But when he went to the island he might meet someone else, and this thought tormented her. This she could not bear.

He would say to her sometimes, 'It's not me you want, it's me as a possession. Can you not see that you're being as rigid as the church you hate? Can you not see that?'

And as she stood there, unforgiving, unyielding, that was what he thought. Yet she thought the same about him, for there was a stubbornness in his nature too.

Now and again he might go off to the pub, which she didn't wish to do. There he might meet some of his island friends, temporarily passing through the city, freed momentarily from their ships. He took a pride in the fact that he could still talk to them as if they were his equals, that he had no 'side'. He would talk to them in Gaelic immediately he met them. All of them had this relationship to the island, it would not leave them be: it was an iron mother. To go back there was like a return to the womb, to those warm waters. It was their mother, their nurse, that ambivalent salt and bitter brine.

I have not changed, he seemed to be saying to them, even though I am a lecturer. I'm still the same boy who fished with you for eels in the rivers, played football, went out with girls.

Damn you, she thought, for your hypocrisy. Of course you're different. What do they know about Welsh poetry, about Irish roots? And she would

70

shout at him out of her great anger, just as if it was her aunt in front of her, risen from the dead in a vigorous blackness.

But he would say to her, 'You don't know Glasgow. You live in one of the better parts of it. You've been protected whether you like it or not.'

Yet she loved the city. She had never really seen violence in it, though certainly there had been some burglaries in the neighbourhood. Glasgow was mobile, it was not frozen in time by the rules of religion.

One night she shouted at him, 'Do you know why you're going back to the island? I'll tell you. It's because you haven't been promoted, and you're not good enough to be a professor. You're willing to turn our lives upside down for that. You're using the excuse to get out of Glasgow and out of the department. John Morrison was right enough. It's the menopause.'

'You shut up,' he shouted at her. 'That tramp. What does he know about anything. It's nothing to do with that. Can't you see? It's because I wish to do something useful. I do not think that what I am doing is really useful, that's the whole point. Yes, if you like me to admit it, I will never be a professor. I have nothing more to do here. What's the point in carrying on in a job that you know is finished? I'm not saying that Morrison, if he likes, can't be interested in his job. That's up to him, I'm not talking about him. I'm talking about *me, me, me!*' And he thrust his face at hers so that for a moment she was reminded of her aunt when she was in one of her frightening rages, so that she could smell the slight tang of rottenness

71

from her teeth. '*Me, me, me!*' shouted Martin, before going out and slamming the door behind him.

Martin's father, a fiercely moustached, aggressively patriotic piper and singer, would remind his son of the history of the island, of the struggles against landlords, of the riots when some of the crofters had marched on the landlord's estate only to be confronted by a silent line of policemen.

'When it suited them they wanted us there, when it didn't they wanted us to emigrate. Never forget that.'

He told his son with satisfaction of the time when raiders killed deer from the estate, and having put up tents with large canvas sails and masts, dined on venison, while grace was delivered by a crofter who thanked God for his bounteous provision!

He told him of the emigrant ships sailing to Halifax in Nova Scotia, bearing their burden of young men. 'It was by the grace of God that I didn't go myself, but you have uncles in Australia, in New Zealand.'

In school, when Martin was given the choice of French or German, his father had said to him, 'What is this French? There isn't a man in the village who didn't think the Germans were better soldiers than the French. The French would cut your throat.'

He was fanatically attached to his croft, stony though it was, and had a boat with which he would go out fishing, teaching his son how to catch mackerel. Sometimes when they were out on the sea he would sing.

'Fàsaidh smal air òr, fàsaidh còimhneach air an aol,
thèid a' ghrian a chòmhdachadh le ceò is le droch thìd,
na lusan 's bòidhch 's an t-sàmhradh bheir an geamhradh
   gu neo bhrìgh
ach gaol far 'n tèid a dhoimhneachadh cha tèid air chall
   an tìm.'

('Rust will grow on the gold, moss will grow on the
   whitewash,
the sun will be surrounded by mist and bad weather,
the plants that are most beautiful in summer the winter will
   bring to nothingness,
but love where it is planted will never be lost.')

And his son would look at his father, handsome, moustached against the sunset, and think of him as a god, master of the elements. And it was from him that he grew so interested in the language.

'Remember, Martin, a people without a language will die. They may not know it, but they will be dead. They will be just like tramps.' And he would ask Martin questions about vocabulary. English was not spoken in the house at all.

'Listen to me,' he would say. 'In some of the islands you will hear people call a peat cutter a *cas chrom*, but that is not true, the real word is *tairsgear*.

'And some people will say *a niste* for "now". That is not right. That is carelessness. You look up the word and it says "nis".'

He told him of the derivations of the place names in the area. 'Now do you know what *Càrnan a' Chnuic Ruaidh* means? Well, I'll tell you. It means Little Cairn of the Red Knoll. This would have been a cairn which would have been built for drying tangle weed when the kelp was being worked. The stone used to build these cairns was said to have been plundered from

73

ancient cells and structures which had stood there for years and years.'

He was a poet in the midst of his ancient poems. Every stone was resonant to him. 'Listen,' he would say to Martin, as he played a *pibroch*. 'This is called "The Lament for the Children". Nothing greater was ever made in the history of Scotland.'

Most times however he didn't speak much of Scotland. The island was the beginning and end of the world to him. Scotland was another country on the far horizon, dim and blue. The sea made for him the most magnificent music of all. Its language was languorous on sunny days, threatening on wintry days, but always present, immediate.

'When I went to Glasgow once, what a hateful place it was. I missed the sea. Till one day I passed a shop that was selling whelks and I felt at home there for the first time. But how men can live there I can't understand. I cannot fathom it at all.'

He was proud of his son when he brought home the prizes for Gaelic (among others). 'Glè mhath, a bhalaich,' he would congratulate him. 'Well done.' Material benefits, promotions, meant nothing to him: he would sing at the local *ceilidhs* for nothing.

'What does a man need that he's not got here?' he would say to Martin.

And he also taught him to fight. 'I don't want a son of mine to be beaten by anyone of his own age.' But in spite of that, Martin was beaten a few times as he was not a fighter though not short of courage, and only his mother saved him from his father's wrath.

'You can't have everything,' she told his father. 'If he's going to be a Gaelic scholar he can't be a fighter as well.' (And his father had bitterly reconciled

74

himself to the fact that his son would, like a bard and historian of old, remain on the edge of the battle in order to report the victories or defeats to others.)

Later, Martin was to wonder how his father had so much knowledge considering that he had left school at the age of fourteen, and had hated school and the master who used to beat them on their bare legs with a leather belt. He concluded that it was because he had a marvellous memory: nothing that ever passed into his head was ever lost. And this was shown most clearly in his knowledge of genealogy.

'And this Mary Nicolson', he would say, 'is the granddaughter of Alex Macleod who used to be a stonemason in this place. His brother was a shoe-maker and a cripple.' And so on.

'I wish your father was alive to see you now,' said his mother the day he left for university. 'How proud he would have been.' (For his father had had a stroke many years before which had left him speechless, and in his later years he didn't know anybody and could not even recognise his own sister. However, near the end he regained the power of his speech and the marvellous thing was that he had reverted entirely to Gaelic.)

How much he owed his mother too, thought Martin. How she had protected him when he had not come up to his father's expectations and ideals. How calmly she would talk to him till his rage died down.

(And later she herself would be lying in the hospital in the town while her son was in Glasgow unable to help her. And it was true enough, she would have died in Glasgow more quickly than at home. For to her and her husband Glasgow was a vast, almost unimaginable city, dark and foggy, far from the sea – for after all what was the Clyde but a dirty little stream from which ships had sailed in the past bearing the emigrants to Canada?)

They had spoken in Gaelic as they parted. And on the ship itself there were members of the crew who spoke in Gaelic, and the islanders in the saloon spoke in Gaelic, but his approach to Aberdeen was marked by a change in language, and for the first time he heard words like 'loon' and 'cauld'. Nor did he fall into the trap of sinking into the dream of *ceilidhs*, for these songs that they sang were not the true traditional songs and their tunes were not the true traditional tunes.

But, in a strange way, he felt that he was sailing away from his father, who sometimes seemed to wave to him from the sea as he stood upright in a small boat, his bald head like a stone in the wind.

'Mar sin leat, a bhalaich,' he bid them, till his voice could not be heard at all.

And in Aberdeen on certain nights when the moon was full, he would think of the island tethered to him like a triangle of light that he could never let go. Oh, these moons of the island with their wandering perfumes, how they would return to him when he least expected them, piercing him to the very roots, with pathos and desire, with the salt of tears and joy. Never before had he realised the smallness of the island, that it was not a whole world.

In his four years at Cambridge, before going to Glasgow and after he had left Aberdeen, what was it about the former city that depressed him? It was perhaps the smartness, the glibness, the artificiality of the wit, the elaboration of language at the expense of feeling. No matter how hard he tried he couldn't imagine his father in Cambridge, though indeed it was a beautiful city with its own history. And once he laughed out loud as he thought of his father punting on the sheltered waters of the Cam, his shirt billowing in the wind. What tracks his tackety boots would have left on those lawns! Sometimes he himself would wake up in the middle of the night wondering, What am I doing here? Among these ex-public schoolboys with their natural poise and self-confidence? Though in fact his own first school had been called a public school . . .

No, he didn't make any friends at all at Cambridge, where he felt as much an exile as he imagined the highland emigrants had felt in Canada. No matter how hard he tried to make friends, there was an intellectual glaze on these people which he could never pierce, a lack of seriousness in the sense that he knew seriousness. (It wasn't until much later that he himself could afford a frivolity that he didn't feel then.) One thing he learned from Cambridge, and that was that he would never be satisfied with the aesthetic, that beyond the aesthetic were ethical demands, even existential ones. That, much more than this seemingly élitist place, his own island was under threat, his own language. And that, however much these people sympathised with the ethnic, for them it was only in the end a game, and their way of life could only exist against a background of sophistication and elaboration.

Never, never in Cambridge, and never among his wide reading in other languages did he feel the tears which he felt when listening to his favourite Gaelic

77

song, 'An Eala Bhan', 'The White Swan', which was a
song set in the First World War, the white swan being
the loved one of whom the soldier was thinking while
in the trenches.

> 'Maggie, don't be sad,
> my dear, though I should die,
> who among human kind
> can live forever?'

> 'We are only here as if on a sojourn
> like the flower of the field growing
> that the showers of the year will lay flat
> and that the sun will not raise again . . . '

Nor indeed was that song one of the great songs –
indeed it might be considered a Gaelic pop song in
a sense – but nevertheless it could make him weep.

> 'Good night then, my dear,
> in your perfumed warm bed,
> may you have quiet sleep
> and a happy healthy awakening.'

> 'I am here in the cold trench
> and in my ears the sound of death
> without hope of surviving with victory . . . '

And in English it didn't have the music or the
pathos of the Gaelic language. So that in Cambridge
they would consider the music itself cheap, rustic: and
yet for him it went to the depths of his being, that
figure in the trenches, the white swan on the clean
water . . . .

★

What a hot summer it was, thought Jean. I must learn to exist on my own again. So at dinner time, instead of eating sandwiches in the office which she had done in the past, she would wander out to the park, which was quite near. Here she would sit on a bench and feed the pigeons, slaty-blue and pompous, and big-chested as councillors, as they strutted with short legs towards the bread which Jean threw. And she would watch the women with their children, the old men with their newspapers and their pipes, the young boys and girls strolling hand in hand towards the adjacent wood with its fine sheltering trees. On the island there were hardly any trees, and she had grown to like trees very much, especially the long shady avenues in Aberdeen, but here too she liked the coolness, the sense of secret growth. The island had hardly any trees except round the white castle with its rhododendrons and its pheasants that wandered like enamelled maps on the ground.

She was conducting an experiment. Can I live on my own again? If Martin goes back to the island can I prepare myself for his departure? And so she talked to people, to old men who told her about their pensions, about their ailments, about wars where they had apparently done astonishing things which had never been recognised. But more especially to one oldish woman with thin legs bunched darkly with veins, who was always carrying a shopping bag weighted with food. The old woman would ease herself down on the bench and say, 'Thank God for the Cooncil. Do you see that wee bugger there?' pointing to a pigeon slightly bigger and busier than the rest. 'He gets everything. See that? The wee bugger,' she would say admiringly. 'You working around here? I used to work here. Use'ta clean the cinema steps when they had cinemas, but now it's all bingo. Use'ta look up at the pictures of stars big as hooses and imagine myself like one of them.' And here she would laugh, the laugh shaking her whole body. 'Clark Gable, Humphrey Bogart, the lot o' them. And I use'ta imagine myself on their airms going to a dinner party in Hollywood, in furs, white furs, I think they were. On cold days, that was. See, I still get arthritis from it. There's nothing so bloody cold as these steps, marble they were. Now it's all bingo. And sometimes the manager would gi'e me a free ticket. All the smoke, you never get smoke like that nooadays, you could hardly see the screen for it. Noo, there's no smoke at all. It's no' the same. In the old days it was like going oot among company, everybody in a' that smoke, noo it's different, you don't get the same idea of being together. I was in one afternoon and I was the only person there, imagine that, not even the kids. It was eerie, I can tell you, sittin there on your tod in the middle of that big cinema; and then the screen's too big. It's different somehow. Tell you something, there was another cinema here and you use'ta get in with jam jars, what do you think of that? Lemon curd for the balcony, and strawberry for the stalls.' And she burst out laughing again. 'And a man use'ta spray you with disinfectant at the interval. 'Course it was all Westerns. But it was everyone together in those days, know what I mean? Not like now. Everything's too clean, too tidy. Where are you from then? The Highlands? A teuchter, eh? I've been there. With my husband on holiday, years and years ago, but there was nothing to do. On Sunday there wasn't even a café open, no chippie, nothing. And you'd think they'd have plenty of fish up there, but no. I wouldn't like to stay there, everyone to himself, but I like Glasgow, wouldn't live anywhere else. That wee buggar, see him stealing from the rest? Big bully, get away from there, gi'e the little ones a chance. I study them a lot, I know which ones are the bullies. Now, my husband, you'd never meet a kinder fellow, but when he had drink in him, look out. He changed just like that, one minute he was laughing and the next minute he was vicious. Funny that. But most of the time he was really nice and he would give you his last penny. He wouldn't do anything the nurses told him at the hospital, he was always opening the windows, couldn't stand being shut in, and that's how he caught his cold, pneumonia it was. Get away, you big bugger. See them, I mean there they are and they just eat bread, but what do they usually do when there's no bread? If there was no bread, that's a puzzler, eh? And see that fellow there in the army coat? He comes every day, and he sits there. I don't think he's got a home to go to, and he never speaks to anyone. I tried to talk to him one day but he just got up and walked away. No manners, no breeding. And I don't know if you've seen his eyes, they burn through you. I like talking to people but that one's defeated me.'

Then the two of them sat in companionable silence, while the pigeons cooed softly around them, coming right up to their legs, to their shoes. Ahead of her, Jean could see the greenhouses with their thousands of foreign exotic plants, ghosts against the glass. She half-listened to the old woman, who was going on like a river.

'. . . and I went and visited them. And do you know what? She practically keeps him locked up. She never speaks to him. You've never seen anything like it. He comes home and he has to give her her wages.

It's as if he was in a prison. She's one of these people who thinks the world of herself, went to America on her own and left him at home, went to the White House she told me and left her handbag on the bus, and she keeps him in there. He told me he had a chest condition but she never bothers, she says it's all fancy, and no' to send for the doctor. People are funny, aren't they? You wouldn't credit it.'

And she laughed self-delightedly. 'Do you know that my doctor has a glass eye? Funny-looking fellow. When he looks at you he's no expression in his eye at all. Just like marble. You know the marbles we had when we were wains? His eye's just like that. And when he comes to see me he says, "And how are you, pet? Your chest OK today? Not given up smoking yet?" And I say, "Of course not. It's the only vice I've got." And he says, "I bet you that's not true." "But why should I give up smoking?" "Quite right," he says to me with his glass eye. "You keep on, pet. After all, as you say, what's the odds?" And the thing is, he smokes himself, not that you see so many doctors smoking nowadays. That's why I hardly ever go to him, you can't smoke in the waiting room. Oh, my God,' and she looked at her watch. 'I'll have to go. The dinner's waiting on me.' And she waddled away like one of the pigeons.

Jean got up from her seat and walked into the wood among the trees where there was coolness and absolute calm. At that moment Martin would be lecturing to his students or perhaps looking up a reference in a book. On a branch above her she saw a small bird perched: it was a wonderful shade of blue. She stood and looked at it for a long time. A poem from her childhood came back into her mind.

'O welcome to thee gentle cuckoo
with your sweet melodious song . . . '

Though of course it wasn't a cuckoo; she didn't
know what bird it was. She didn't even know the
names of the trees, whether they were beeches, elms,
oaks. In a short while she would have to be going
back to the office. The leaves of the trees sparkled
around her like waves of the sea and she could see
areas of blue skies between them. The sound of her
feet was lost in the silence of the wood.

And then quite suddenly – was it a dream, a
nightmare, did it happen at all? – there he was in front
of her, the man with the trench coat, throwing it back,
and she could see his penis throbbing, red as fire, a
snake pulsing out of the wood. His expression was
triumphant, as if he were saying, Look at that, look at
that, that is the centre of it all. He had thrown his head
back and was laughing directly at her. He was holding
his penis in his hand as if he would spray water from it
like a hose. The hardness of it, the triumphant power,
she almost fainted, she couldn't run away from it, and
then she found she was running, and she could hear
his laughter, his mad laughter, as he perhaps scuttled
back to the bench again, though in fact there was no
one there, no one feeding the pigeons, the benches
were deserted, and in the distance she could see the
black gates and was terrified lest they might be locked.
But when she looked back he wasn't coming after her
at all; there was only the silence of the wood, and still
she ran, her handbag bouncing against her thigh, as
she made for the gates which, thank God, were open,
and walked out into the street, slowing down, even
seeing a policeman on the other side of the street,
but not going over to him, so dreamlike the whole

83

episode had been, as if it hadn't happened at all, the benches deserted as people returned to their work. And certainly he hadn't been on any of the benches, the man in the trench coat; he must still be in the wood, and that throbbing flesh, hard and barbarous, oh God, she must not tell the others in the office, she must be calm, otherwise they might think there was something wrong with her, and even now the scent of the flowers around her from that wood, so strong, so powerful, even as she walked along the street and saw the white-gloved policeman directing the cars at the traffic lights.

But nevertheless she had to go home early that afternoon, however much she tried to act normally. Her face was so white, and she couldn't concentrate, and they told her, 'You must be worrying, look after yourself, we can't have you coming down with sickness.' But all that night she couldn't stop seeing the man like a bird of prey opening his wings, floating towards her, laughing, laughing . . .

'You OK?' said Martin, looking up from his book.

'Yes, I'm OK.'

'Are you sure? You look white.'

But for some reason she didn't want to tell him, though he was gentle and considerate enough. That island throbbed between them. And he came over, and she rested her head on his shoulder as in the past, till suddenly she said, 'I must go and make some tea.' Sometimes she believed that he had already begun to live on the island. She had heard him on the phone the night before, but he wouldn't tell her who he had been talking to.

It was true too that he had begun to live on the

island. He heard again the sound of the sea, he smelt again the rank scent of the flowers, he fished in the startlingly blue lochs. His father stretched his hands out towards him from a boat burning in fire, against mountains cut like cardboard against the sky; there were moons round as cheeses, there were dances. He touched the lambs, the sheep, the dog nuzzled his hand, the heather spread mile after mile in waves of purple. Am I entering the communal dream? he thought, Is this what is happening to the mocking one? But the details were clear and fine: the ring of daisies around the house, the smoke climbing into the sky, the cows mooing and haphazardly chewing the clothes on the clothes line, the old men sitting by the fire smoking pipes, and himself rolling and rolling down a brae towards a stream and landing in the water. And his father saying to him, I don't want a Macdonald beating my son. Or remember your people, remember them, they were hunted like sheep, like deer. And he sometimes saw the words of the language itself like little daisies just in the edge of the horizon, dawning there . . .

And again and again he heard the words of an old woman whom he had talked to when he was home at the funeral of his mother and who had actually been a friend of his mother's. 'Nothing in this village, a *ghràidh*, but Dutchmen and Englishmen. They buy the houses, it's like being in a desert. I don't know anyone here, not a single person. It's not like the days when myself and your mother used to go to the fishing, five pounds we got for three months' work, and we lived on herring; that was in Yarmouth, and one day we were standing by the sea, and shells began exploding there; the German ships had escaped from Scapa Flow. Nothing here but Dutchmen, and some of them weave on looms – did you know that? – and they cut peats and they like doing it, they think it's a great thing, and hardly anyone else cuts peats now. And I was a maid in a house and I got three shillings a week, and I had to walk three miles every morning and back in the evening, no cars then, no buses, in rain or shine. And so you're Chrissie's boy, and you're a lecturer now in a university. And how proud your mother was of you, how proud, only she always wanted you to come home, but she would never say. A proud woman your mother, and your father, a *ghràidh*, there wasn't anything about this place he didn't know. A clever man that, *duine tùrail*.'

One afternoon when Martin was strolling idly down Byres road, having been to the library, he ran into Gloria Summers who was a student in his classes, though in fact she was older than the others.

'Hallo, and should I call you sir,' she said, half mockingly, drawing back from him with parcels in her hands.

'Hallo,' said Martin abstractedly. 'I've been to the library.'

'Well,' she said, 'you can come up for a cup of coffee, if you like. My flat is just round the corner.'

Martin thought for a moment and then said, 'OK'.

As they walked, he carrying her parcels, he asked her how she was getting along with her studies.

'I like the literary side, not so much the linguistic.' She was tall and blonde, perhaps in her late thirties, Martin calculated. Had her husband died or were they divorced? He had some idea in his mind that she was a single parent.

'Exactly the way I felt when I was in university,'

said Martin, remembering his professor who had been both a dedicated philologist and golfer.

They climbed some stairs together. She fumbled in her bag for a key and finally opened the door. The flat was not a large one. From some room music was emanating.

'That'll be Sheila,' said Gloria, putting down her parcels. 'My daughter. The school's on strike, so she's home all day.'

A young girl of perhaps fourteen appeared to greet Martin politely, and thereafter sit on the sofa. She wore a green blouse and jeans.

'Her spelling isn't so good,' said her mother, 'but otherwise she's not so bad apart from her English. I've been half thinking of getting her a tutor. Because of the strikes she's missing a lot of schooling.'

While her mother was putting the groceries away, Martin talked to Sheila.

'Have you not got a good English teacher?' he asked.

'Well, she's not good at keeping control. Otherwise I like her.'

'What are you doing?'

'Oh, we do the usual stuff, D.H. Lawrence, *1984*, and so on. I have difficulty in keeping the characters in my head.'

'How do you mean?'

'We have to do character sketches. I have difficulty in doing them.'

She was a well-mannered, open-faced girl. Martin liked her immediately.

While they were talking her mother brought in coffee for the three of them.

'I see you two have got acquainted,' she said.

'Yes,' said Martin. 'We were talking about her

school books. And, by the way, what will you do yourself when you get your degree?'

'Oh, I thought of teaching somewhere on the islands. I've always wanted to go there.'

'Why?' said Martin, drinking his coffee.

'Oh, the peace I suppose. One gets so fed up of the cities. You see, I am divorced. I married too young and didn't know what Ch– what my husband was like. He bet a lot on the horses and I had to supply him with money. Then he went out with other women.' She paused with the cup in her lap. 'I've always wanted a simpler life, not so hectic. I was brought up, believe it or not, on a farm in Ayrshire.'

'I see,' said Martin, thinking. The grand illusion, the simple life, the pastoral life. 'There's certainly one thing, there aren't many betting shops on the islands.'

'I'm sure not,' said Gloria. 'As a matter of fact I let Sheila here see her father, though she doesn't like him much.'

'How would you like the islands?' said Martin to Sheila.

Sheila shrugged her shoulders and smiled. 'I don't know. I might miss the city. I don't know.'

'She wouldn't at all,' said her mother. 'She's just saying that. She actually has few friends here. On the islands she would have more friends, I'm sure. In any case, the islands are a better place to bring children up in.'

'I suppose so, in general,' said Martin, thinking of his wife. 'There's certainly less traffic, cleaner air.'

'And in any case,' said Gloria, 'I've thought of them in a romantic sort of way. I've read so much about them. I've been trying to teach Sheila here some Gaelic.'

88

'Trying,' said Sheila, smiling, so that Martin felt pleased by her innocence, her friendliness, her politeness.

'As a matter of fact there are other reasons why I want to leave Glasgow,' said Gloria. 'More coffee? But these are more private. For a start, I want to get further away from Charles.'

'The cost of living would be higher on the islands. You do know that?' said Martin.

'Yes, I know that, but I would have a job. At the moment I have a grant, but it's not easy.'

Suddenly Martin came to a decision. 'I'll have to be getting along,' he said, then added, 'I could come and give Sheila some lessons, if you like. What time is she available?'

Sheila glanced at her mother who said, 'Usually about five. She could make a point of being here any night you wished. For an hour or so, I take it.'

'As a matter of fact I could give her a crash course every night for an hour or so. I could be here at seven. Seven till eight would suit me fine.'

'That's very good of you,' said Gloria. 'Very good indeed. How much . . . ' she said hesitantly.

Martin waved her away. 'Nothing at all,' he said, 'it would be a pleasure.'

'Well, thank you,' said Gloria. 'Thank you indeed. It's most kind of you.'

'Not at all. Thank you for the coffee. I'll see you tomorrow night, Sheila. Which shall it be?' he said lightly, 'Shall I teach you Gaelic or English?'

'English,' said her mother, 'if you don't mind. She doesn't do Gaelic in the school and in any case I can teach her some myself.'

'That's fine,' said Martin. 'At your service. Have your books ready then, Sheila,' he said.

'Thank you very much,' said Sheila, glancing at her mother.

As he and Gloria stood at the door outside the flat she said, 'The fact is, she's a lonely child. And of course at the moment we don't have much money. But are you sure you will be able to come along so often?'

'Of course I can,' said Martin airily. 'Of course. I like her. She's a nice girl.'

'Yes, but quiet. She doesn't tell me what goes on at the school, for instance.'

'At that age it's their innocence that appeals,' said Martin.

'Yes,' said Gloria sadly, 'isn't it?'

Why did I volunteer to do that? Martin asked himself as he walked along Byres Road. For the life of him he couldn't understand it. Was it so that he could be near Gloria? He didn't think that was the answer. Was it so that he could train himself to teach at a lower level? He didn't think it was that either. He felt extraordinarily happy as if he had made a good decision. What, however, should he tell Jean? Should he tell her that he was teaching English to a thirteen- or fourteen-year-old?

He decided that he would not tell her, but that he would say he had work to do at the university at nights. This was the first time in his life he had deceived her, if it was deception. It was however as if this was a secret that he needed to keep. He felt as if life was beginning again; he couldn't account for it.

He turned up at the flat every night, as he had promised, at seven o'clock, and during the day found himself looking forward to the visit. Nor was the irony that he was teaching the girl English lost on him. It was as if he were entering a quiet almost religious room far from the traffic of the world. They studied *1984* together, for this was the book that fourth-year pupils most commonly did. He told her the background to the book, the concept of history as erasure. She listened to him intently, though he wondered whether she understood what he was saying.

He wondered what sort of life she herself had led. She and her mother didn't have much money. The furniture wasn't new; he imagined her mother buying it carefully in second-hand shops. Yet the girl herself was neatly dressed: and had been brought up well and with good manners. She would even ask him if he wanted a cup of coffee. 'No,' he would say, 'we must press on with the book.'

'Do you understand the idea of erasure?' he would say to her. 'There is a man in a picture with other dignitaries and then he is blotted out for ever. That is history.' Her own father hadn't been completely blotted out by her mother.

Sometimes her mother would be in the room, sometimes not.

'I think I do,' Sheila would say. 'Do you mean that they changed everything?'

'Yes, every book they wrote would be destroyed, would be taken away from libraries. It would be as if they had never been.'

The girl was present to him, alive, the world was still ahead of her. And as for him, was the world still ahead of him? But at least he knew that he could teach her age group, which he hadn't been sure of before. It was also refreshing to turn to this book after the grammar and philology which he had taught before.

'And language too,' he said. 'Language was Newspeak. Do you understand that? The language itself can be changed.'

'I don't understand that so well,' she said, staring intently at him.

'It's like this,' he said. 'Do you see that sofa? What colour is it?'

'Green,' she said.

'Well, what if someone else said it was red? If everyone else said it was red? Would you still stand out and say it was green? Would you not begin to have doubts?'

'I don't know,' she said, biting her lips and making an effort to understand.

'You would begin to doubt, would you not, if someone came in and casually referred to it as red, and others did the same? And the same of course with ideas.'

'I don't know,' she said doubtfully.

'It's not as simple as a lie,' he said. 'In a lie you know that there is a truth you are not telling. Here it is different. Here everyone has been conditioned to saying, "This is red, this is red, this is red", and why are we so absurd as to believe the opposite?'

But she couldn't quite get it. 'It's like this,' he said. 'If you had been brought up on the island where I was brought up, a lot of people go to church. Why do they go to church? Not because they are holy. They go to church because the others go to church. Do you understand? If they don't go to church they feel there is something wrong with them. And the ones who go to church despise the ones who don't as if they have a secret of their own.'

She understood secrets, and suddenly her eyes lighted up. It was as if she were among her kind and some of the girls had a secret which it was necessary to share. She said so, and he answered, 'That is like it. And eventually because you want to get into the secret you will be willing to believe anything. It would have been no use as in the days of Joan of Arc to send someone to their death believing in their own ideas. That would only be the death of the body. What they are after is the death of the mind, you understand. They must make Smith believe in what they say. To kill him while he still believed in his own ideas was no use. And that is why they used not physical but psychological methods.'

She raised her head at the word 'psychological'. And he continued: 'They could have shot him, burned him to death, but that wouldn't have made him change his mind. So they used the rats. Imagine it.'

She shuddered.

'The rats at the cradle,' he said.

She shuddered again.

'We'd better have a coffee,' he said.

While they were having coffee he asked her about school. She didn't seem to have many friends. She liked some of her teachers and disliked others. She played the flute in the school orchestra. All the time he was talking to her he was aware of an independence, a coolness that troubled him. It was as if she had learned in the circumstances of her family to rely totally on herself. It was a characteristic that he had noted in her mother as well. Like a vase, he thought, like a fragile vase.

He thought of leaving some money but decided against it. He thought it would be an insult. His

93

mother was always giving money to people, not only to tinkers but to relatives of the dead for buying food for the wake, or for the meal after the funeral.

'Do you have no close friends at all?' he asked Sheila.

'Well, there's Julie.'

It turned out that Julie was an upper-classish girl whose mother had almost sent her to a private school but who had decided against it at the last moment. She rode horses and spent her time grooming them. He sensed that Sheila wanted to be like her, envied her.

'Julie doesn't care about the teachers,' she said. 'She talks, and goes her own way. The teachers give her rows but she doesn't care. She laughs a lot. Miss Dupres hates her.'

'Why?' said her mother.

'Miss Dupres is French and Julie imitates the way she talks English.'

'But that's wrong,' said her mother.

'It's very funny,' said Sheila, laughing at the memory of it. 'She does talk English funny.'

Martin drank some more coffee. He found himself drinking a lot of coffee in this flat. At home Jean was silent a great deal of the time, as if wondering what the two of them were to do, but thinking that they had come to an impasse. It was as if she waited for a solution which time itself would provide. She never talked about the office now at all: it didn't seem to matter to her that he was going out every night. He noticed that she was wearing darker clothes than usual. Was she preparing for their divorce? Was this her mourning for their marriage?

As for himself he knew that Gloria's reason for going to the island was a wrong one. To go to the islands for work was the correct reason. And it was

possible that his work with Sheila was a preparation
for his migration there. Sometimes he would look at
her geometry books and see the triangles as images
for the island to which he was returning, bare and
demanding without foliage. Even in his university
room he would stare out of the window as if he
had come to the end of a journey in himself.

As he walked home after his sessions with Sheila it
was as if he were walking through a graveyard. The
city no longer had any meaning for him, it echoed
posthumously with his footsteps. He remembered the
girl's intent gaze at him, her youthfulness, her air of a
future. Was this purpose of returning to the island a
disguise for something deeper? He wasn't sure. And
yet at the same time he felt that his own work was
on the island, that his father and mother were pulling
him back.

He talked to Gloria about his childhood, about his
youth on the island. He told her that he intended to
resign from the university.

'I want to go back', he said, 'because I have
outlived my usefulness here.'

'Oh, I wouldn't say that,' she said.

'I know what is happening perfectly well,' he said.
'I am existing on my past at the moment. I am like a
record spinning long after the music has finished.'

'And I want to go there', she said, 'because I
want to be part of its history, of its tradition.'

'I want to go there because of a future,' he said.

'Oh, that too. I would try and get a job in one of the
primary schools. I would be quite happy there. After a
while I think Sheila would be happy too. I think what
happened in my marriage was that I became nervous
of the gap that had suddenly opened. You see, I
had high expectations of marriage. I believed that

marriage lasts for ever. I got that idea, my husband used to say, from pop records, from Elvis Presley.'

'I see,' he said. He had never listened to Elvis Presley.

'In fact,' she said, 'I suppose I want to go to the island for security.'

But that wasn't his reason. He wanted to return because it was the last chance for his language, because of the insults that it had suffered, because of the many exiles, the many dead, the waste. But how could he tell her that? It wasn't in her bones, in her blood.

'Thanks for the coffee,' he said, and left. Big Brother is watching you, he said to himself, as he watched his shadow cast on the wall of the tenement in his descent.

Jean knew perfectly well that Martin was not working late (since she had once or twice phoned the university) but was not concerned with him betraying her with another woman – his island conscience was such that he would not do that. She thought that perhaps he was meeting some of his sailor friends in a bar or even that he was walking about the city wondering what he should do, perhaps in a strange way saying goodbye to it, for he had a more sentimental sense of place than she had. She didn't raise any objections nor ask any questions when he left the house, perhaps hoping that he might still change his mind about going to the island and that these hours spent away from her were for the purpose of clearing his head, of finding at last a fixed street among many. Nor were her calls to the university a spying on him, they were simply the result of phone calls to him by other people.

Her own work at the office continued. It was possible that if he left, this work would become more important to her than before, and to tell the truth she found among the other women a certain sanity which comforted her. And it was mainly to safeguard her future that she agreed to go to Daphne's flat one night to meet some people.

'Just a few,' Daphne said, smiling. 'And, by the way, bring a photograph of Martin.'

'A photograph?' she said.

'If you can manage,' said Daphne.

Thus on a Tuesday night she found herself outside Daphne's flat with a photograph of Martin in her handbag, though what she was carrying it for she didn't know. It was a photograph of him in his university robes just after he had graduated and he was smiling hopefully into the future.

It occurred to her that when she was ushered into the flat by a Daphne dressed glamorously in a long blue dress, the occupants were all women – she thought about four, at a hasty glance. She was introduced to all of them and vaguely ticketed in her mind a Muriel, a Flora, a Norma, and a Catriona. They swam about her in their fine colours.

'Sit down here', said Daphne, 'and have some coffee.' The others nodded to her and then talked among each other.

As she drank her coffee Daphne said, 'Jean here doesn't know anything about our Tuesday meetings.' (What have I got into here, thought Jean, a witches' coven?) 'It's all very simple,' said Daphne. 'We meet here because we are all divorcees.'

'Oh,' said Jean, and for the first time she felt

a coldness as if she were already separated from Martin.

'We comfort each other by telling stories about our exes,' Daphne continued. 'That is all. Muriel here was just telling us about her husband who is a doctor. You can just carry on, Muriel.'

Muriel looked shy and awkward at first, but then went on. 'Oh, it was just that he took me for granted. He didn't attack me or anything like that.' Her small precise body, clad in black, became bitter and her voice almost singsong as if she had told the story before.

'He would get these postcards, apparently from a friend called Hugh who, he said, was a fellow student with him when he was at university. Only it looked to me as if the handwriting was that of a woman. So I followed him one night in the car – we had two cars – and sure enough he met her outside the cinema. His Hugh was a dress designer called Thora.'

She sat for a while staring into space, and then said, 'Eventually we got a divorce. Do you know that after I had got a place to live he came one night and took away a vase which his mother had given us as a wedding present?'

'I found exactly the same,' said a woman in a red dress. ('That is Flora,' whispered Daphne.) 'I mean about property. Jeff was mad about it. He couldn't bear any of his property being touched. Even when I was cleaning the rooms. I think it must have been his poverty when he was young – he was one of five children. Even his jogging suit – he took up jogging, would you believe it? – he couldn't bear me to touch them. "Leave them as they are!" he would shout. "Just leave them." And so we had slanging matches because I am tidy by nature.' (As she spoke she moved a coffee cup from one side of the tray to the other.) 'He said I should have been a spinster; perhaps I should have been. And that was how my marriage broke up. I couldn't bear it, that he should be throwing his clothes on the floor all the time. He would leave his ties hanging across chairs. It actually gave me a headache. When he left, though, the house looked tidy but empty. I remember it very well. It was very quiet. But he could easily have been tidier than he was,' she said, raising her eyes to the others. 'It isn't difficult to be tidy.'

'No, indeed,' said Daphne sympathetically.

'It was the taking of the vase that got me,' said Muriel, her face ugly, her mouth precisely shut like a purse.

'It wasn't untidiness with me,' said the third one, dressed in a blouse and green skirt. 'He just couldn't stand my mother.' ('This is Catriona,' whispered Daphne.) 'Maybe I shouldn't have brought her into the house at the time, but what could I do? She was old, infirm. But she was very demanding. He wouldn't make any allowances for her at all. Of course she didn't want him to move the plants in the garden, she wanted them to stay as they had always been, which was natural enough, and she would make a fuss. But then one has to make allowances, doesn't one? I suppose if it had been his mother it would have been different. It was different with his mother. He used to visit her regularly, at the expense of the children. She used to fill the heads of the children with all sorts of rubbish.

' "You old bag!" he shouted at my mother one day. Of course she had hysterics, and that was the beginning of the end. "Clear out!" I shouted at him,

99

but then it was his house. "You clear out!" he shouted. So we had to find a small dilapidated flat and we lived there for a year, till my mother died. He could have been much more reasonable, but he wasn't at all reasonable. Not at all.'

By this time Daphne had taken out a bottle of wine and was pouring the wine into glasses. 'So you see,' she said to Jean, 'I had this idea, we would all meet and discuss our marriages, not to save them, that's too late, but to show how much we hate men. Men are vicious,' she said, the bottle shaking in her hand. 'They are children. They want what they can get immediately.' Her face was suddenly contorted with rage.

'And now for you,' she said to Jean. 'What has your husband done to you?'

'What?' said Jean, nonplussed. 'Martin?'

'Well, what has he done to you?'

'Done?' she said impulsively. 'He wants to go home to the islands, that's what. And I don't. That's all.'

'But he puts himself first,' said Daphne.

'In a way he does, I suppose.'

'The fact is,' said Daphne to the others, 'he wants to return home and leave Jean here because she doesn't want to go.'

It looked to Jean as if Daphne had been drinking before she took the wine. She looked around her at the ring of intent faces.

'Take a drink,' said Daphne. 'Go on.'

'I'm not sure that I— ' said Jean.

'Go on. Everyone here drinks.'

Jean noticed that one of the women, the one who hadn't told her story – Norma, was it? – a tall girl with glasses, was pouring out some wine for herself with a trembling hand.

100

'Norma here,' said Daphne, as if following the direction of Jean's gaze, 'was beaten up by her husband, weren't you, Norma?'

Norma remained silent, and Daphne said, 'He was a dentist, would you believe it, and he said he hated the infliction of pain, but he beat her up regularly.'

Norma stared down at her glass sadly.

'Well, then,' said Daphne, turning away, 'tell us about Martin.'

'There's nothing to tell,' said Jean. 'I told you. He wants to go and teach in the islands. And I don't want to go.'

'Why don't you?' said Muriel, bluntly.

'I just don't want to,' said Jean. 'I don't like it there.'

'Why not?' Muriel insisted.

'I was brought up by an aunt and I didn't like her. You see,' she said, 'I am illegitimate.'

Strangely enough, she brought the word out without pain, without unease.

'Of course not,' said Flora.

'Of course not,' they all said, drinking their wine. 'Why should you like her?' It didn't seem as if illegitimacy was a concept that bothered them. In the clear wine Jean saw the image of her unknown father swimming, tiny, distant.

What am I doing here, she thought, saying these things about Martin? After all, does he deserve them? Among these embittered women.

'Shit,' said Daphne suddenly, banging the table and almost upsetting the glasses which tinkled against each other. 'We all know what men are like. Do you know what my husband did to me? He said to me on a Tuesday at nine o'clock, "I'm walking out and I'm not coming back." Just like that. I didn't even know there was another woman. He had his case ready in

101

the hall. Just like that,' and she tossed off a glass of wine in one gulp, and went to open another bottle. 'My best friend too, whom I met every day at work. So I had to leave my job as well. I still see the bitch now and again. Men,' she said, 'you can't believe a word the buggers say.'

'No, you can't,' said Muriel. 'They're all liars.'

'He has told me what he wants to do,' said Jean helplessly.

'Yes, but he still intends to go ahead, doesn't he?' said Daphne. 'That's the point.'

'The whole point,' said Catriona, the one whose mother had been disliked by her husband. There was a stain on her dress where her shaking hand had spilt the wine. Norma was staring ahead of her through her large round glasses, looking like a schoolmistress trying to focus on a blackboard.

'Have you brought the photograph?' said Daphne to Jean.

'Yes, though I don't know what you want it for.'

'We'll put it up with the others,' said Daphne, 'won't we, girls?'

For the first time Jean noticed that behind her on the wall were photographs of five men, one of whom wore glasses (perhaps that one is the doctor, she thought, or the dentist).

Daphne took the photograph from her and pinned it up alongside the others and at the same time Jean felt the headache beginning in her right eye. Oh, God, she thought, not another of these. The pain rayed from her eye to the back of her head and down her nostril. She put her finger to her eyeball, which felt tender.

Maybe I shouldn't have taken that wine, she thought. I'm sure I shouldn't have. The photograph of Martin stared at her optimistically and innocently from among the others.

'It's not too early for the ceremony!' Daphne shouted.

'No!' the others shouted back.

Daphne walked over to a case which lay on a table near the window and from it removed six darts, one of which she gave to everyone. The five walked over to a corner of the floor which was free from furniture, and lined up beside each other.

'Come on, Jean,' said Daphne, 'here's your dart. What you have to do is throw it at Martin. You can do that, can't you?'

From the small Muriel to the tall Catriona they looked like a firing squad.

'Give the bastards hell!' shouted Daphne, drawing back her dart.

No, no, thought Jean, I don't want to do it. I don't hate Martin that much. I will not do it. She picked up her handbag and made for the door.

'Hey, where are you going?' shouted Daphne. 'Where are you going?'

Jean's head was bursting with pain, rays emanating from all directions in it. There was a throb in her right eye, a needle probing sadistically. She imagined the pupil of her eye as a bowl inside which her diminished aunt knitted steadily and calmly.

'What's wrong?' shouted Daphne from the head of the stairs.

But Jean kept going till she was on the road again. She headed steadily into the night tilting with lights, putting her hand to her right eye as if she had been wounded, as if she were returning from a battlefield.

Why the hell did I leave the photograph there?

103

she thought, through her pain. I should have taken it with me. Muriel's face, bitter and locked, slanted towards her. Next, a head with tall glasses stared down at her.

Oh, God, the pain, she thought. Something is happening to me. My aunt is sticking needles in my eye. The city itself was multi-coloured. She walked steadily on, her eye throbbing, stabbed by a raw red pain.

Martin, Martin, where are you? I did not mean to betray you. You have a right to do what you wish. You have been good to me. And the rays were a sunrise in her head.

One night Martin took young Sheila to the fair. His feelings for her were hard to explain: it was as if he thought of her as his daughter, fresh and bright, one to whom he could show the world or what he knew of the world. They were not at all carnal, they were entirely virginal. He had noticed that neither she nor her mother had much money, so he insisted on paying for the outing himself. I have all this money, he thought, which I earn from work that I don't like doing, so why shouldn't I spend it?

Sheila enjoyed the fair very much. He took her on the dipper, and she screamed as they rotated above the bright lights and the people. He and Jean had once been on the dipper in Vienna used in the film *The Third Man*: it was a slow stately dipper and he had looked over the city absent-mindedly while Jean, who did not like heights, turned away from the window.

Now he and Sheila were on the dipper, and later they shot with flawed guns at targets. Sheila did not shoot very well, but he won a doll which he gave her. It was a small rag doll with glass eyes, pauperish, not attractive. However, he noticed that Sheila clutched it lovingly to her breast. They also had ice-cream. And they watched a big, mountainous woman in a tent, the fattest woman in the world. A mass of flesh, she sat on her seat as on a throne. A freak. A terrible, sorrowful shaking hill.

He watched Sheila with a consuming interest. She seemed very self-contained, as if she were maintaining some inner secret. Perhaps her life had been, after all, an unhappy one. She reminded him at times of Jean; she appeared to be one of the ones who had learned about pain when young. It was as if he wanted to give her more than was possible. And yet this fair was ramshackle, cheap, shoddy. Perhaps he should have taken her to the theatre. But when he suggested this to her she said she would rather the fair. They spun pennies. They sped down the Haunted Tunnel while skulls, green as moss, shone in front of them. And even then she didn't scream, as he imagined other girls might have. Nor did the distorting mirrors frighten her as she became tall and thin, fat and squat, as her face elongated and widened.

The fair was bracelets and necklaces of lights; there were paintings of wolves on the sides of the machines. And, tall and distant, Sheila moved among it all. If only she were my daughter, thought Martin, she is so cool, so self-possessed.

Once she volunteered, 'My daddy used to shoot.'

'Oh,' said Martin.

'Yes, he was in a club. He used to shoot clay pigeons. He said I was no good.'

And she didn't say anything else about him.

Martin was suddenly jealous of this father, whom he had never seen.

'I was no good.' The words echoed in his mind. There was so much that he wished to tell her, to teach her. That was what he was above all, a teacher. But she had such a crystal fineness, such fragility. A vase. A tall slim vase.

'Such a lot of litter,' he said angrily at one point, as he looked down at the ground where there were papers of all kinds, including half-eaten packets of fish and chips. The place was so dirty, so third-rate. He was angry with Glasgow for its untidiness; he wanted cleanliness such as he remembered from the island. There was such a casual tawdriness in this city.

'Can you give me ten p,' a man in a stained jacket said to him. He had come up without his noticing. 'I don't know where I slept last night. I don't know where I'll sleep tonight.' His breath was an alcoholic fume.

Martin put his hand in his pocket and gave him the 10p. 'Thanks, mister.' The man staggered off, while Sheila gazed pityingly after him. Maybe he should shout him back and give him some more money, but he had disappeared among the crowd. An old woman suddenly swore at him, 'Look where you're going, you effing clown!' Her voice was like a seagull's, pitched high with fury and venom.

Don't touch me, she seemed to be saying. Don't touch me. Martin glanced at Sheila, but she didn't seem to be frightened. Martin hated to hear women swearing, perhaps because of his upbringing.

This cool, cool girl, this daughter he might have had. And the fair spinning round him, coloured, dizzying, shoddy. These rotating wheels, these imperfect guns, these third-rate prizes. For a moment it seemed to be a reflection of life. And yet there was a curious warmth about it, a slapdash glory as of a child splashing paint on paper at an untidy kitchen table. And the music was incessant.

'Are you enjoying yourself?' he asked Sheila.

'Oh, yes,' she breathed. And her eyes were shining. So that he suddenly felt himself king, would have given more money earned from his perjured job to give her joy, as if his whole mission in life were simply that, to confer happiness. As if he were a transparent window through which light would be cast on her. So this was what fatherhood was like, to be transparent.

She was curiously at ease with him, he knew that. She accepted him casually without strain. He had not had the pain of bringing her up, but she turned to him as a friend. So too must Jean have been, distant, self-contained, but with possibilities of warmth. And he thought of her with spurts of love trying to be affectionate to her aunt and being rejected. How much was done to the children of the world!

'Are you frightened of the city?' he asked her.

'Frightened?' She didn't understand.

And yet was it fear of the city that was impelling himself home to the island? He thought about it. No, not fear, more a sense of the unfinished, of the untidy.

He remembered travelling on a train with a man sitting in front of him, a complete stranger to him. There they sat for two hours not speaking to each other, not knowing how to get in contact with each other. How odd it was! The accommodations necessary to survive with people in a city. The *Gemeinschaft* ... was that the right word?

'Come on, then,' he said, almost roughly, to Sheila, and the two of them left the fair and the noisy tunes which he did not know.

'Don't forget your safety belt,' he told her at the car. My daughter, oh my daughter.

'Thank you very much,' she said in the same self-contained polite manner.

'Oh, that's OK,' he said.

No, it wasn't fear he felt, only the raggedness of things. Or was it that he had no family? Perhaps that was all it was. If he had had a family would he have been content to do without his ideals, would he have been forced to do without them? Would the family have been enough? The mind was so complicated, how could one plumb its depths?

He had a vision of being out with Jean and Sheila, all of them together, a family. Then the vision faded as Sheila stood, Cinderella-like, on the doorstep saying good night.

'Thank you very much again.'

In Glasgow this tall crystal vase, breakable. Breaking his heart.

'Good night,' he said. 'Take care.'

But by that time the door had shut on her and he was driving up Byres Road. It was too early for Jean to have gone to bed. How could he ever explain to her what he was doing? It was simpler to remain silent. For language was the origin of complications.

'I don't know why you are doing this anyway,' said Jean, as she checked that there was enough drink in the cabinet.

'It was simply an idea,' said Martin. Perhaps it was a silly idea; maybe he was trying to get these people

108

to make up his mind for him. He glanced through the window into the garden, which looked wild and untended. Really, he should spend more time on it.

'Nina takes vodka,' said Jean absent-mindedly, 'and Calum takes whisky, isn't that right?'

'I think so,' said Martin.

'And this singer you met, what was his name again?'

'Norman. He'll take whisky, I'm sure. His wife – by the way her name is Jessie – will take vodka or sherry, I should imagine. I don't really know though. I've never met her.'

Jean muttered something under her breath. Then aloud she said, 'I bet you Nina will arrive first.'

But it wasn't Nina who arrived first, it was Calum, resplendent in kilt and green jacket, as he often appeared when chairing *ceilidhs* in the city hall. He was a big man with a bald shining head. When he sat down he spread his legs, smoothed his kilt, so that one could see his thighs.

'Whisky,' he said, in answer to Martin's question. And then, 'I've been hearing things about you.'

'Such as,' said Martin.

'Oh, things. That you're thinking of going back to the island. Lucky man.'

'I haven't decided yet,' said Martin, glancing at Jean who sat down on the sofa.

'Water?'

'No, thanks. Never drown a good whisky. Is this malt?' he asked, sniffing.

'Yes. It's Glenfiddich.'

'Very good. And how are you both?'

'Fine,' said Martin, watching Calum smooth his sporran.

'I would go back there myself but you know Nora, she wouldn't go.'

109

'Why not?' said Jean abruptly.

'She doesn't like it up there. To tell you the truth, when we were married, or just after, I took her home to the island, and there were no toilets in those days. It was very embarrassing. Not that it bothered me. But Nora wasn't used to it. I tell her there are plenty of toilets now, electric light, and what have you, but she won't go. So what can I do?'

'That's true,' said Jean, looking at Martin.

'For myself, as you know, I'd go back tomorrow. But then in a way I think I'm doing good work here with the *ceilihs* as . . . Oh, there's Nina. I can see her coming up the path. Dressed to the nines.'

Martin hurried to the door before Nina could ring the bell. The other two could hear a faint conversation. Then Nina came in followed by Martin. She was wearing a long blue dress and a blue shawl, which Martin took from her as she entered.

'Well, well,' said Calum, lumbering to his feet. 'Long time no see. How are you, Nina?'

'Fine,' said Nina, sitting in a chair near the sofa on which Calum and Jean were sitting.

'Vodka, please,' she said to Martin. 'With tonic.'

'Your grandfather knew it well,' said Calum with a laugh. 'Vodka and tonic water.'

'Were you up in the island yourself?' said Nina, smoothing her dress.

'No, not at all. I haven't been up for two years now. Sometimes I go there on my own,' he said to Martin apologetically. 'I do some fishing. There are some fine lochs. But I hardly know anyone there now.'

'I find the same,' said Nina. 'Exactly the same. It's not the same. The warmth has gone.'

'I find more warmth at the city *ceilidhs*,' said Calum expansively.

'You feel you are doing something important,' said Martin in a voice so neutral that the question didn't appear like one.

'I must say I do. Oh, I know that the proceedings are often in English and we are criticised for that. But what can we do? The fact is that non-Gaelic-speaking people work hard for the cause.'

'The cause,' said Martin ironically, as if there were inverted commas round the words.

'We have to learn to compromise, you know,' said Calum, leaning back comfortably. 'If we didn't compromise we might just have a few people.'

'The songs,' said Nina. 'There's nothing like the old songs.' Her haggard face seemed to become misty and vague.

'We have a singer coming tonight,' said Martin. 'He's a young singer.'

'Oh, what's his name?' Calum enquired. 'Do I know him?'

'I don't know whether he's sung at your *ceilidhs*,' said Martin. 'I met him by chance. He works at the shipyard. He hasn't been long in Glasgow.'

'Which island is he from?' said Calum.

'Oh, your own. Raws. I believe he's quite a good singer.'

'What's his name?'

'Norman. Norman Macaulay.'

Calum brooded for a while, smoothing his sporran, but couldn't think of a singer of that name who had sung at any of his *ceilidhs*.

'I'm surprised he isn't here,' said Martin, glancing at his watch. 'I said eight o'clock.'

'Anyway,' said Calum, 'if you leave the university and go back to Raws to teach will you not be taking a drop in salary?'

111

'Yes,' said Martin tersely.

'Is that a wise thing? I mean what does Jean think of it?'

'It's his decision,' said Jean, without explanation. Her statement was as bare as the island.

'Yes, well . . . that's good,' said Calum. 'Nora would have words to say to me if I did that. Things are so expensive.'

'And more so in the island,' said Nina. 'I was reading in the paper the other day that a basket of goods is far more expensive on the island than it is in Glasgow.'

'That's the freight of course,' said Calum. 'You have to pay for living on the island.'

'But think,' said Nina, leaning forward, 'when we were growing up there was no inflation. Prices seemed to stay the same all the time.'

'I think that was an illusion,' said Martin.

'I don't think it was. I think the prices did really stay the same for years. Now it's all different.'

'I must say I admire you,' said Calum, but before he could finish there was a ring at the doorbell.

'That'll be Norman and his wife now,' said Martin. 'Her name by the way is Jessie.'

Norman was a dark squat young man with black hair. His wife Jessie was tall and blonde and willowy: she wore white slacks and a white jacket. She carried a white purse. Calum stood up and bent low over her hand.

'Well, well,' he said to Martin, 'you never told us she was such a good-looking girl. She's a stunner.'

Norman glowered. 'Whisky,' he said to Martin, who had asked him what he wanted.

Martin had the idea that he had been drinking before he came.

'And Jessie?'

'Cinzano, please, if you have it. With lemonade.' She simpered.

'Oh, yes, we have it,' said Martin.

'Now then, Jessie, come and sit beside me here,' said Calum, patting the sofa beside him. Norman glared at him but said nothing. He sat on a chair.

'I hear you're a singer,' said Calum. 'You must come and sing at our *ceilidhs*.'

'I don't sing much now,' said Norman in a cold voice, from which every word fell like a large stone.

'Oh, if you have the talent you should use it,' said Nina. 'If I could sing in public I would do so.'

'But you only sing in your bath, eh, Nina,' said Calum.

Jessie giggled and then put her hand over her mouth. Norman glanced at her with a thunderous expression.

'Norman works on the shipyards,' she said. 'He has different shifts,' she said, as if this explained why he didn't sing much in public.

Calum patted her hand.

'Yes, you defend your husband. Quite right. Have you been long away from the island, Norman?'

'Not long.'

'About two months,' said Jessie.

'Are you liking it here?'

'Yes,' said Jessie. 'Very much.'

'Why is that, now?'

Jessie clasped her hands together as if looking for inspiration.

And Nina said, 'The Sundays will be cheerier anyway.'

'That's right,' said Jessie.

'One thing I didn't like about Raws was the

113

Sundays,' Nina continued. 'I had a cousin of mine from the island here with me recently and he wouldn't watch the TV on a Sunday, and he wouldn't let me read the Sunday papers. I didn't like that about Raws.'

'It was going to extremes, that,' said Calum, 'I must admit.'

'And you couldn't even dance, they objected to that,' said Jessie in a daring torrent of words.

Suddenly Jean got up and walked over to the record player. 'I think we should have some music,' she said, as she selected a record. The black disc spun and the song began,

'Peggy my love you have left me completely without joy,
As I sail across the sea to Australia . . .'

'That's Calum Kennedy,' said Nina. 'He's a lovely singer.' Her head rocked from side to side and now and again she took another sip of her vodka.

'Yes,' said Calum. 'A strong singer. Did you know he had won a medal in Moscow?'

'Is that right?' said Nina. 'I didn't know that.'

('. . . and I up above keeping her on course . . .')

'So many of our songs are sad,' said Nina. 'I wonder why that is.'

'Not at all,' said Calum vehemently. 'Not at all. I could give you a lot of songs that aren't sad. That's an illusion. What do you think, Jessie?'

'I agree with you,' Jessie simpered, clutching her handbag.

'I knew she would agree with me,' said Calum, looking around the assembled company in triumph.

Martin passed round more drink. There was a

steady hum of conversation, like the noise made by grasshoppers in the evening. Norman sat by himself glowering, now and again glancing at his wife. Martin was sure that he had been drinking before he came in.

'There was a poem we had in school when I was young,' said Nina. 'It was called "The Cuckoo". It went:

> 'O fàilt ort fèin, a chuthag ghorm,
> le d'òran ceòlmhor milis . . . '

We used to have to learn it off by heart. And then the master beat us if we didn't know it. Why, he used to lash at our bare legs with his strap.'

'But he gave you a good education just the same,' said Calum.

'And I'll tell you another thing,' said Nina. 'He would beat you if you spoke a word of Gaelic in the school.'

She sipped her vodka, remembering, her face red with anger.

'I left Raws because there was nothing to do,' said Norman, as if dropping a stone into a pool. 'My father wanted me to stay and look after the croft, didn't he, Jessie, but there was nothing to do. The church . . . ' And he almost spat on the floor.

'There's more to do in Glasgow, right enough,' his wife simpered.

'I'm sure there is,' said Calum.

The first record had come to an end and, with a quick glance at her husband, Jean put on 'The Bachelor Song',

> 'Iain a luaidh nach pòs thu?'
>
> ('Iain, my dear, why don't you get married?')

115

'Now that's a cheerful song,' said Calum. 'That's a nice cheerful song.'

'That's right,' said Nina. 'John was very fond of that song. John was my husband,' she said to Jessie. 'He loved Glasgow. He was very popular. He was going back to Raws when he retired. But it wasn't to be.' She looked as if she were about to cry.

'And that's why,' she suddenly shouted to Calum, 'I sit at the window knitting and watching the buses.'

'I'm sure you're a good knitter,' said Calum. 'You'll have to make me a jersey one of these days.'

'You wouldn't wear a jersey with that outfit,' said Nina smartly.

'It was never the dress of the Highlander anyway,' said Norman stonily. 'No Highlander wore that stuff.' His speech had become slightly slurred.

'There's nothing wrong with a kilt if you have the legs for it,' said Calum, winking at Jessie, who simpered. 'Anyway I have to go to the place.' And he levered himself upright from the sofa.

'His wife,' said Nina curtly, when he had gone. 'Who was she anyway to be offended by lack of toilets? She comes from Hamilton. I'm sure she lived in a room and kitchen up a close. And yet when you see her on the platform in her furs you would think she was God almighty.'

'You watch it,' Martin heard Norman whispering fiercely to his wife, who turned away as if embarrassed.

Nina muttered to herself. 'Putting on airs. Skempy,' she added.

As Calum came back from the toilet he stopped beside Jean and glanced at the records.

'Put on "Eilidh"' he said. ' "Eilidh" is a good waltz tune.' The black disc began to spin.

116

'There is a difficult road to the mountains of the
island . . . '

Suddenly he pulled Jessie from her seat and began
to waltz with her round the room, almost bumping
into a sideboard full of glasses.

'Watch what you're doing,' Nina shouted, putting
her hands over her eyes. Wiping his eyes from the
sweat, Calum gave Jessie one last turn and then
collapsed on the sofa, his legs spread wide.

'That's against the law,' Nina shouted. 'I can
see your drawers.'

'Come on,' said Norman to his wife. 'We're going.'

'Already?' said Martin.

'Already?' said Calum.

'Come on,' said Norman. 'That old fart is beginning
to bug me!'

He took Jessie by the hand, placed his empty glass
down on his chair, and the two of them left while
Calum stared after them in amazement and shock.

Suddenly Nina began to laugh. 'You should see
your face,' she said to Calum. 'I thought you were
going to have a stroke.'

Calum spluttered. 'Such ignorance, such ignorance.
I didn't mean anything. It was just a bit of fun. What's
wrong with the fellow?'

'I think he's probably drunk,' said Jean, from
her station at the record player.

'The way he spoke to me,' said Calum. 'I would
never have said that in company. Is that what they're
learning on the island now? I didn't do him any harm.
I've a good mind to phone the police.'

'That wouldn't do any good,' said Martin. 'I'm
sorry about it, but it really wouldn't. I think he'd
been drinking before he came in.'

Nina was still spluttering with laughter. She could hardly get her words out.

'Your face,' she said to Calum. 'I've never seen anything like it. It was as red as a beetroot, and there you were in your kilt with your legs spread, and he said that to you. They're a new breed, right enough.'

Yes, I was shocked, thought Martin, but really why should I have been? Should one respect one's elders even when they aren't worthy of respect?

The music suddenly came to a stop and Jean took off the record, and there was an uneasy silence.

'That's the trouble with these singers,' said Calum. 'I've seen it time and time again. They come from nowhere and then they win a medal and they act like lords. I've had a lot of trouble with them in the past.'

He was like a great coloured ship sinking slowly but still trying its best to keep afloat.

'I think', said Nina, 'that he was nervous After all, Martin here is a lecturer and . . . ' She stopped.

'You mean it was a social thing,' Martin prompted.

'Yes, I think that's what it was. After all . . . One of our singers told me that when she went home she missed the warmth she used to find, because they would say to her, "Oh, you're a famous singer now. This place must be too dull for you."'

'What singer was that?' said Calum, surfacing from his harassed sea.

'I think it was Morag MacNeill. I can't remember. Anyway, that's what she said. Will you miss Glasgow?' she suddenly said to Jean.

'I don't know yet whether I'll leave Glasgow,' Jean replied.

'You mean . . . ' said Nina, her eyes glittering.

'You mean that Martin might go up there on his own?'

'I don't know yet,' said Jean. 'I like Glasgow. I didn't use to like it but I do now.'

'I used to like Glasgow when John was alive but not now,' said Nina.

'Would you like Raws any better?' asked Jean.

'I don't know. I really don't know.' She held out her glass humbly for vodka like a beggar. It was a simple heart-breaking gesture. Martin filled her glass with the transparent fiery liquor.

'I hadn't thought of that,' she said to Jean. 'I hadn't thought of that. I came to Glasgow because John had a job here. I didn't want to leave the island. I was only twenty-one. We took the ship and then the train. When I arrived in the city I wanted to run away. It was in the forties. I thought it was the ugliest place I had ever seen in my life. Nothing but ruined slums. For a long time I would hardly go out of the house. I cried all the time. If it hadn't been for John I don't know what I would have done. But it was his livelihood and he loved being a policeman. He never got any promotion but the people liked him. They knew he was fair. Teuchter they used to call him. He would polish his boots and badge till they shone. He missed the police when he fell ill, and he was always hanging about the police station. Anyway, that's the way it was.'

'Yes, he was a good man,' said Calum in an odd voice.

'I used to be ill when I came here first,' Nina continued. 'I thought I would never get used to the city. But there was one woman, a Catholic she was, funnily enough, I made friends with. She was Irish. She was a nice woman. Once or twice I even went to the chapel with her.'

119

Martin looked out the window and saw John Morrison staggering up the drive. He went to the door, opened it, and shouted, 'Get the hell out of here and don't come back! I'm busy.'

John's mouth opened in amazement, and then quite docilely he turned on his heel and swayed back the way he had come. Martin felt a fierce joy scouring his whole body. This is the night for revelations, he thought. This is the night for the shedding of illusions. This is the night for truth. No more yellow, heavy, romantic moons; let us have the clear sun of truth, the frosty one that lies on the horizon like a crystal globe.

'Was that John Morrison?' said Calum.

'Yes,' said Martin tersely.

'He's a good scholar,' said Calum. 'But they say he drinks heavily. Did you know that he gatecrashed a talk the other day and started shouting at the lecturer? I was never so ashamed.'

He is the worst, thought Martin, the one who has been infected by the city, the one who has been poisoned by it. The lost one. The doomed, clever one. And yet he was not sorry for what he had done. And the dreadful thing was that Morrison would return as if nothing had happened.

'Well,' said Calum, 'this won't do at all. I'll have to be going. It's half past nine. I'll have to work tomorrow.'

What is his work again? thought Martin. I can't remember. And then he did. Calum was a lawyer and apparently a good one too.

When he had come in from seeing Calum to the door, the phone rang.

'It's for you,' said Jean, 'it's a woman's voice.' Martin took the phone from her hand, as Nina chose that moment to leave as well. As he listened to the voice at the other end, he felt unreal. Nina turned the corner. The shaking voice was still speaking. He glanced at his watch. It was, as Calum had said, half past nine.

As he drove away from the house, Jean beside him (for she had insisted on coming, though she did not know yet what was going on) Martin thought, Something must have happened to her. He was only half listening to Jean who, in an angry muffled voice, was saying 'Who is this Sheila?'

'She is a girl I was teaching,' he said, his eyes fixed on the road, while part of him was thinking, How is she not home at this time of night? And he saw her as if directly in front of him, wandering the late-night streets of Glasgow, stretching out her arms to him, saying, Help me, please help.

'I was teaching her,' he said. 'Her mother's name is Gloria.'

Jean's lips, he imagined, were locked like a purse, and as he glanced at her sideways, he thought, Why, at this moment she looks as her aunt must have looked once to her, prim, disapproving, pouting like a child, and yet at the same time he also thought, With good reason, for she knew nothing about this, and about my affection for this young girl whom perhaps I see as my own daughter, now lost and sullenly wandering this city. And he thought of the city as like the skeleton of a map which, like an explorer of old, he must wander, hoping not to find what perhaps he must find. Lord knows what he might find, and now and again there were flashes of Sheila, tall and fair-haired, in front of the car, beseeching him to help her. And Jean beside him now shrunk into silence, visibly smaller, her face fixed on the road ahead of her, not wishing to speak to him at all, and in front of him the yellow lights blooming on the tops of the lampposts, like unsleeping flowers, surrounded by a halo of mist, those flowers which on first coming to the city he had hated, though not in their first intimations of pink, certainly in their more flagrant yellow.

Jean followed him up the stairs while he knocked on the door of Gloria's flat. She answered the door, looking at Jean almost with surprise, and then in reply to his question, 'Have you phoned the police?' said she had, but so far there had been no information. A girl in Sheila's class had said that there was a collection for Action Aid, for relief to Ethiopia, and Sheila had no money, and had silently blushed. Then, when the classes were over, she had thought that Sheila would be going home as usual. She had no reason to think otherwise, but she had certainly looked pale and distraught, especially as she was one of the few, perhaps the only one, who had been unable to contribute.

'She had no money, you see, I don't know,' said Gloria. 'You see,' she said, speaking this time directly to Jean, so much more shrunken than her, 'I'm divorced, and I . . . I should really have been working, but I had this dream of going to the Highlands; the fact is that I hate the city. I get a grant from the Education Department: I thought I would learn Gaelic and then I would get a job up there and settle there.' (All the time Jean was looking at her, distraught and blonde and beautiful, as if she were her mortal enemy.) 'Anyway, I know why she didn't have much money, but enough for her dinner and so on . . . '

And her voice faded away.

Then she began again. 'But I did teach her to have respect for others, to be kind, and this must have been what disturbed her, for she has a vivid imagination, and she must have thought of these children in Ethiopia dying, and she didn't have any money to give them. I can understand it; you see, she saw them, these pictures on the TV . . . '

And again she stopped, and then suddenly, 'You don't think there was anything between Martin and me, do you? I hope not – it's just that he was teaching Sheila because he . . . I think it was because he wanted to learn to teach children again, at least that was what I understood . . . '

Jean didn't speak, looking at her as if trying to understand what was happening, so that for a moment she looked like a pouting disappointed child herself in the sparsely furnished living-room with its second-hand suite, sofa and two chairs in a pale, scarred green.

'I know it looks odd,' said Martin briskly, 'but I simply offered to teach Sheila, and then another time I took her to the fair.'

'You see,' said Gloria, 'I am learning Gaelic. I have always wanted to go and live in the Highlands – how can I put it? – ever since I first read about Prince Charles. I was always a reading child, and then there were other things, the peace, the silence. It's been hard in the city with no husband, looking after the child . . . '

And she glanced at the phone, as if willing it to ring. 'I'm so frightened.' And she shuddered. 'I'm so frightened. What she might do . . . . Teenagers. How they see the world. So tragic.'

'This won't do at all,' said Martin briskly. 'We can't sit about here. We'll have to go and look for her. We'll take the car.'

And it was as if his sudden decisiveness had gal-
vanised the other two, especially Gloria, into life, for
they followed him quickly and obediently downstairs
on to the street to the front of the tenement where his
oldish red car was parked. He glanced at his watch, 'It
is now eleven o'clock.'

'And it's not as if we knew anyone in Glasgow,
I mean we don't have any relations,' said Gloria, as
she got into the back of the car, leaving Jean to get
into the front. 'I mean she has school friends, but not
to visit, not to stay with.' (Still Jean wasn't speaking,
silently looking from one to the other as if she were
trying to decipher a difficult manuscript.)

'She liked Martin,' said Gloria, 'she said that
he spoke to her like an adult.' (She is much more
beautiful than me, Jean thought, with that careless
beauty that does not draw attention to itself, the
blonde hair, the greenish, I think, eyes, the almost
sculptured face with its very fine bones. Was it just
Sheila, then, Martin was interested in? And she looked
straight ahead of her at the lighted streets.)

'Where are we going?' said Gloria.

'We'll tour the streets,' said Martin.

And that was what they did. There were still a
number of people on the streets, emerging noisily out
of pubs, shouting, singing, swaying, saying their last
good nights, linking arms, women clip-clopping on
high heels, men staggering a little, joking, laughing,
slapping each other on the backs, in the dapple of
yellow and red lights.

And then once a tall man in a long black cloak
talking animatedly to a small girl wearing, Jean could
have sworn, black lipstick, while the youth looked
around him haughtily like a demonic actor, swinging
a cane with a leisurely air.

124

And a tall young man, unshaven, standing at a lamppost, while a smaller, older man was tugging at him and arguing with him, the smaller man also unshaven, and his face red and angry, and the young man suddenly taking him by the throat and shouting at him as if saying, I don't want to be bothered by you any more. Clear off.

I never really got used to the city, Martin was thinking. It was disparate, nothing had any connection with anything else except by simultaneity, by random simultaneity. There was always something hostile in it, there was no warmth, as I had when I was young, strangeness, serendipity, all these but no unity such as there was in the island where I grew up. How can I explain it? A feeling that in my very bowels I have been an exile, no matter how much at times I like the city, there has been a lack of . . . a lack of . . . centre, of meaning; it is a moving kaleidoscope but it has nothing to do with me at all, the deepest me. Is this, too, a matter of language? And yet the city has its language, its winking semaphore, its signs, its advertisements, its alphabet which is not mine, which is alien to me.

And Jean was still thinking, I don't understand what is happening. Yet I am interested, I am interested in finding this girl though I have never met her.

'I hope you understand', Gloria was saying, 'my obsession with the Highlands. It's . . . I kept thinking that something would happen to Sheila, that she would get into drugs, into drink. I wished to protect her, and then I thought of that place, so peaceful, so serene. It's been quite hard on one's own, and then, Martin, you see, seeing the best side of Sheila, naturally on her best behaviour, but like all teenagers she could be difficult. She was saying she wanted to leave school, take a job, we never had any money . . . '

Martin was hardly listening to her, and now and again he would see a young girl walking by herself, and he would slow the car down, and the young girl would look at him in a frightened manner as if she thought he was going to attack her, but it was never Sheila, not Sheila with her tall assured walk, but a different face altogether, pale, slashed with lipstick, seen momentarily and then past.

But Jean was not saying anything, still staring ahead of her, like a judge, like her aunt possibly, and yet there was also an interest there, a gleam, as if she was slowly beginning to wake up, to think . . .

Past closed offices the car ran, past shops, past telephone kiosks, past post-boxes, past statues, gardens, and he suddenly thought of that vase which they had, the one of Orpheus and Eurydice, and now and again it was as if he saw Sheila turning, looking at him, with her unendurable youth, as if about to speak, and then not knowing what to say; while in the back Gloria was saying, 'We should have stayed, perhaps . . . the police might have got in touch with us; maybe we should have stayed at the phone.'

And Jean thinking, It is like, it is like he is looking for me. I am lost in the city, and he is looking for me, but unlike him I love the city. I love him too. I know, yes, I am sure, I know that he didn't betray me, but on the other hand what do we know about other people, even the ones we love the most, and when I think of it my whole body melts with fear and rage, my head crackles with anger. I am alone here, alone, walking . . .

Now there were not so many people on the street, which began to look almost shuttered and desolate except that now and again there would be a single person, usually a man, walking along, his heels clicking on the stone.

And Gloria saying at the back, 'God knows what she's done. She may have . . . God knows. Or whom she may have met.'

It was as if he had been driving for ever, in circle after circle, searching for the girl at the centre of the labyrinth, as once in Aberdeen he had tried to get through the maze, and youthful voices were heard in the maze, and boys and girls danced in and out of it, and he was trapped in it, trying to unlock its secret by the power of the intellect alone, whereas that was not what was necessary at all, but only an intuitive almost uncaring instinct as he had once in his youth, or thought he had.

'We will never find her.' Gloria was weeping quietly in the back, and for the first time Jean spoke.

'We will find her,' she said. And Gloria was suddenly grateful to her, more than she could say, and ceased to weep, as if Jean's voice had calmed her and she was now certain that Sheila would be all right, only saying very quietly that she hoped she had kept away from the water. She was always highly strung, though you wouldn't think of that to look at her.

'We might as well go back,' said Martin at last. 'She might be home by now.' And he swung his car round in the middle of the road, and they drove back in silence, seeing fewer and fewer people on the road, for the city was awesomely silent, an empty place. Down Great Western Road Martin drove, round by the Botanic Gardens, at which Jean gave a shuddering look, then along Byres Road, and to the flat, where he stopped the car. But there was no one outside the close, as he had perhaps hoped, and the outer door of the close was shut. They all got out, still in the same silence. Martin pulled the door back, and they climbed the stairs, and there she was, huddled outside the door waiting, having presumably no key. They all stared at her as if she had risen from the dead, and rushed towards her, even Jean, and she looked up and cried, and her mother embraced her, kneeling down, Jean having for a moment seen that face, pale and miserable, but also startlingly beautiful in its vulnerability.

'Where *have* you been?' said Gloria, rocking her daughter in her arms backwards and forwards.

And it came out easily after they were in the flat that she had looked in her purse for money when the appeal for Action Aid came and she had found she had no money at all, and she couldn't forget these children, since she had seen them on television, and the shame of not being able to contribute anything had built up during the day, and she had simply walked away from the school when the school day was over, and she had walked and walked, and she was very tired.

But where had she been?

'Just walking. Now and again sitting on a bench in a park.'

And there was a woman who sat beside her and had given her a sandwich, and then an old man had taken her to his flat for a cup of tea, though she hadn't wanted to go. And the man had a burn on one side of his face and he had muttered to himself, over and over, 'Bloody hell,' as he had fumbled among the dishes, and he had told her that his wife had died recently of cancer.

And at one stage she had stood on top of a bridge and had contemplated . . .

And with her head of helmeted gold she sat on the old sofa and said with a laugh, 'There was this woman, and I walked beside her for a while, and she said she had a parrot and she had taught it to say, "Mrs Thatcher is a . . . "', and she couldn't bring herself to say the word but giggled uncontrollably. The woman had a hat like a bird's nest and was quite crazy, and she had worn tons of lipstick and rouge though she was quite old.

What a walk it had been. And she had not been at all frightened, but angry and ashamed, fuelled by her rage, but all the time it had been an enchanted walk, and she had walked with a drunk man who had talked about Rangers all the time, and had said awful things about the Fenians, and who had eventually stood at traffic lights waiting to cross, cursing the green man, and had pulled out wads of money and told her to take some of it, but she wouldn't, and eventually he had got angry, and crossed against the lights while cars blared about him.

Eventually in the living-room she fell asleep, and Martin made a signal to Jean and they left and went to the car, Jean still silent, Martin staring straight ahead of him and saying,

'I just liked teaching her, that's all. You can see she's a lovable girl . . . '

'Yes,' said Jean, in a small voice, 'I can see that.' And she believed it, she believed that Sheila was the only attraction, having seen her.

'But why didn't you tell me?' she asked.

'I don't know. It was a secret, I suppose. I don't know why I didn't.'

And later in the large kitchen she made coffee while Martin said, 'I can't get it out of my head.'

'What?'

'That young fellow saying that to Calum. It was so unexpected. And Calum looked stunned. I didn't think he was like that at all, he seemed so quiet, and yet he was so . . . he must have been jealous, that must have been what it was.'

'Yes,' said Jean, 'it was funny.'

'It was as if Calum collapsed,' said Martin, laughing. 'It was as if he fell apart. I can't explain it, like blasphemy in church, it was . . . ' And he began to laugh again, helplessly.

'So un-Highland,' he said, wiping his eyes. And he rolled about in his chair while Jean looked at him.

'I mean', he said, 'the community, and that sort of thing, and . . . I could almost hear glass breaking when he said that. Did you not?'

'It was odd,' she said.

'But', he insisted, 'it was more than odd, it was as if a civilisation had come to an end. And Calum sat there in his kilt with his legs spread apart, so open to the world, and he almost looked unprotected, and this young fellow blew it all apart, and the look on Calum's face, I . . . '

And again he went into paroxysms of laughter.

Then, much more soberly, 'It is so complicated, everything is so complicated. Why are we forced to be what we are? To grow into such complications, like snakes always twining themselves around us, this guilt . . . it never leaves us.'

'No,' she agreed.

'Why can't we be simply ourselves?' he said. 'Just ordinary people, like Calum,' and he burst out laughing.

And she thought, Well, why can't we? Why can't I forget that I am illegitimate? It's because I wasn't wanted, I never felt anyone wanted me, that quick moment of penetration and then a lifetime of paying for it. So disgusting. And she shuddered.

There was a time when, for example, she had been enjoying herself at a dinner table and she had got up as if saying to herself, I don't deserve this, I don't deserve anything. Not to have a true name, a true label, to be an aberration, treated as if she were a pariah, when it was not her fault – and that football player whom she had never known drifting in his fine bones about the sea somewhere.

'The guilt,' he said again, and pulled the curtains wide, to show the white moon in its perfect circle, stationary in the sky, a stainless ball, so distant, so pure.

'I remember you in that art gallery,' he said suddenly, 'and you looked so . . . lost, as if that was not your place, so dressed too, I can't remember, I remember thinking you looked so rustic, and you probably thought you were so svelte. Anyway, you were standing in front of that picture and I could see your reflection in the glass, and I went over and spoke to you, and you looked so astonished, just like Calum, as if I had broken an eternal silence.'

'I loved the gallery,' she said quietly.

'Yes, it was so quiet. And we never had one in Raws. I missed that and music, I mean classical music. We were so deprived. Really so deprived. In every way.'

'I used to go there because the paintings were so beautiful,' she said in a distant voice. 'Such colour, you see.'

'I understand. And then I gave that book to the landlady and she seemed so astonished. I had followed you, all the way to your house. You looked such an orphan; we have always been orphans in the city. Like when they first came, the emigrants, they had to work by clocks, they had to clock in. That must have done something to them, and the ugliness after these lovely hills . . .

'I mean this island standing up in the sea like a question mark,' he said, pacing up and down, 'what is it asking, what does it demand of us?'

'What?' she said.

(And she could hear her aunt's voice, What we've done for you, and you treat us like this. We've given you a bed, haven't we? And we didn't have to, did we? And food we've given you. And yet you're so disobedient. Remember who and what you are. Your father didn't care for you. And so on and so on. And she had found a photograph of the football team in the library in the town, in an old newspaper, and it showed her father sitting down among a lot of other players, and the ball was at his feet, perhaps he had been the team captain, and he was looking straight at the camera and laughing, and he hadn't even known that she existed.)

'I don't know why we had all these people in anyway,' she said.

'A lot of them become policemen,' he said, as if he hadn't heard her. 'There must be a reason for that. The rooting out of sin . . . rather than crime. It is natural, I suppose. And yet, unlike you, I was so happy. The sunsets, the red skies, the warm summer nights – never again will I feel that.'

And suddenly he banged the table. 'And look at how we were treated. The emigrant ships. All those people sailing away in their new suits and caps. I saw a photograph recently at an exhibition. It was as if they were setting out on an adventure.'

132

'Yet some of them come back,' she said, 'wearing tartan caps, and they love it, their new country, their superiority, as if they were the rich visiting the poor. I see a lot of them in my job, I speak to a lot of them too.'

'In the middle of their days,' he said seriously.

'Once there was a particular night,' he said. 'I was standing outside our house and I was listening to the melodeon being played at the end of the road, and the moon was in the sky, the autumn moon, and it was all red, I thought of it like a red hen brooding over the earth, and I could hear the thumping of the feet on the road. The moon that ripens the barley, that brings me home to Raws . . . '

She thought, Every night we kneeled on the floor while the old man opened the Bible and put on his glasses and read out a portion of the Bible, sometimes stumbling over the words, and she could have sworn that once he had read out a whole list of names from the Bible, all in the same unvarying voice, and she had kept her eyes open and stared around her, sometimes almost giggling when she saw his bald head in front of her, and her spectacled aunt had rested her head on her arms, and she could hear the grandfather clock ticking as if it would never stop, as if the day would never end.

'Do you know,' she heard herself saying, 'one night I heard my aunt and a friend of hers saying, "What was that man talking about the starving millions of India for? And showing us that film in the church hall. That wasn't the true Gospel."'

But he was thinking of an April, shy and vulnerable, and the shadows passing over and over the ground, and the flowers swaying, the snowdrops, the crocuses; it was like the language itself seeking to live, while the wind passes over it, the wind from eternity, the wind he had heard on the headlands whining mercilessly for ever.

An April day of sun and shade, ambiguous, double, with the cold in it and at the same time the first trembling shimmerings of heat.

Yet sitting in the middle of it, as in an Elizabethan picture he had seen once, showing a young man standing aesthetically among a lot of flowers, Calum in his sunset kilt, and that young voice smashing at him, 'You old fart!' and Calum collapsing back on the sofa with his outspread legs and his suddenly red face.

'Bed,' he suddenly said. And Jean said, 'All right,' and together they went to bed, and for a long time he lay awake watching that moon, monkish and pure in the sky, dazzling, questioning, a ball such as once he might have thrown over a fence in the dusk of a Raws evening.

In the classroom, on the Monday after Martin had finished his lecture on the poetry of Duncan Ban Macintyre, and especially 'Ben Dorain', Gloria came to speak to him.

'I thought it would be good manners to tell you,' she said, 'I'm giving up the course.'

'But . . . ' he began, 'you're doing so well. Are you worried about your progress, is that it?'

'No, it's not that. I've decided to get a job. You see, that incident with Sheila taught me a lesson.'

For a moment he was panic-stricken; she wasn't going to take Sheila away, was she? He felt suddenly bereft; and he looked at the blackboard on which he had written in his quick, almost illegible handwriting,

'"Ben Dorain" is a sort of praise poem, though it is about deer,' and the words seemed somehow remote.

'The grant isn't enough,' she said, 'we've been living from day to day, and then Sheila didn't have any money, that's why she wandered the streets. I can't let it happen again, you do see that, don't you? It's nothing to do with you. I was indulging myself. It wasn't really Sheila I was thinking about, it was myself. I had this dream, you see, ever since I was quite young. I used to read a lot about Bonnie Prince Charles and I thought that there was a possibility of loyalty, romance.'

And at that moment, he could have told her, Bonnie Prince Charles wasn't like that at all. He was an evil ghost who had drifted into the Highlands, like some kind of vaporous poison, with his powdered hair and his boyish rapacity for adventure, intoxicated by the new air, the mountains, the lochs, the heather, and by his selfish opportunism he had brought tragedy on the Highlands. And later he was cruel, a wife-beating drunkard, after he had destroyed the Highlands in a storm of hailstones and fire.

But he didn't say that.

On the contrary, he said, 'Are you sure? Will you be able to get a job?'

'I think I might. I can easily do secretarial work. Something like that. And in any case Sheila wouldn't want to go to the Highlands. I was deceiving myself there too. She wants to be where she is. You see, I've been thinking a lot about it.' And she turned her lovely face towards him, shaking her hair.

'There was Sheila and there are the Ethiopian children, and she couldn't help them because I didn't have any money. It wasn't just romanticism,' she went on. 'I wanted to take her away from here. The school she's in is quite good but it has elements of violence; a pupil attacked a teacher the other day, butted him in the head, that sort of thing. I thought I would be able to take her away from that. But what I was really thinking about was myself.'

'Does this mean you might be moving?' Martin said.

'It depends. It depends where I can get a job. I don't want to move at this moment because it would interrupt Sheila's examinations. But . . . ' and she shook her head.

Martin looked round him at the desk, the blackboard with its almost illegible scribbles like flashes of lightning, the books, the cupboard with its files, the windows with their small panes, and smelt the smell of varnish as he had once done when he had gone to his first class in Aberdeen University, the lecturer there being a small, stout, tweedy man who smoked a pipe.

'Is she all right, Sheila I mean?'

'Oh, she's fine, she thinks it was a great adventure, but I'll have to give her more pocket-money in future. She wasn't at all frightened wandering the streets; the people she met were kind to her. One man offered, she was telling me last night, to get a taxi for her. The poorest people, she said, were the kindest. It has given her something to talk about to her schoolfriends.'

'Yes, of course.'

'In any case, I think you have an idealistic view of her. She can be quick tempered, you know, and moody, and she doesn't do as much work for her examinations as I would like. I sometimes see her writing an essay while she's watching the TV at the same time. I don't know how she can do that, I always need quiet and privacy when I'm working. And she can sometimes be very ungrateful. And also it disturbs me that she didn't think it was appalling for that boy to have attacked that teacher like that. He deserved it, she said, he was a bully, he was sarcastic and always picking on the boy. I said that didn't justify what he had done. He'll only be suspended for a short time anyway.'

If I should lose her, my daughter, thought Martin.

'And then your wife came into the house that night, and I was so ashamed. You see, the sofa is scarred, I don't know what happened to it, it looks as if people had a knife fight all around it,' – she smiled – 'I was so ashamed. What she must have thought.'

'She didn't think anything. I'm sure she never noticed,' said Martin absently.

'But Sheila does. She says we can't invite people to the house because the furniture is in that condition. I'm surprised she is like that considering her attitude to her own things; she leaves them scattered about her room. And I think she would like to invite some of her schoolfriends, only she can't do that. Though I'm not sure if she has many, she is so cool, so reserved. The fact is they're a different race, they're different from us. For instance she eats lots of crisps and chips and lemonade, they exist on nothing. And one night, out of the blue, we had this argument about nuclear war, and she was saying "What's the use of doing anything? We're going to be destroyed anyway." And I want her to do well in her exams, to give her a chance of getting a job. I've this nightmare of her not being able to get a job, and it's quite possible. Sheila tells me of friends of friends of hers who haven't worked since they left school. I suppose I thought of going to the Highlands because it might not be so bad there if you didn't have a job. But of course it would be just the same as here.

I did enjoy the course, the discussions, but it was all really a dream. And in any case, I think it would be better if Sheila went to your house for her lessons, if you're still wanting to do them with her.'

'That will be all right,' said Martin. 'Of course I'll do them.'

'Well, then . . . '

Through the window he could see the greenery of the trees, light, youthful, airy, and some students carrying books in their hands, walking from one classroom to another, some in cloaks – and it suddenly brought back with a pang his own student days and nights, the irresponsibility of them, the debates in that coffee shop, the name of the proprietor which he could not remember but who spoke French and German and was more like a lecturer himself, aristocratic, dapper and alert, and the apple trees at the back of the café, with the sunlight slanting on them; the discussions about Sartre, Camus, existentialism – even though his study was Celtic – the nights of walking home over empty streets with the stunning moon in the sky above them.

'So, I thought', Gloria was saying, 'I couldn't very well combine a job and my studies. It would be impossible.'

Of course it would be impossible.

And then there were his digs, with the little old man who used to sniff his breath when he came in at night to see if he had been drinking, and the statue of Byron just opposite his digs, in front of the grammar school. He wondered where these people were now, the old man, the son, the daughter: the old man would certainly

138

be dead, and perhaps the daughter and son as well.

'Thank you for telling me.'

'Well, then.' And she was gone.

He suddenly banged his fist on the desk. Why should this happen to people, this taking of decisions, these paradoxes, these contradictions, conflicts? There was a Gaelic broadcaster he knew who didn't bring up his children to speak Gaelic. 'It's just that I can't make them, can I?' he would say. 'They've been brought up in the city, they don't want to speak Gaelic. I would like them to, but they follow their peers. And I know what people are saying about me. Everything is pretty complicated.'

To start off from the beginning, like everyone else, without that burden, that would be a good thing, wouldn't it?

And his mother not dying in his house, but . . .

And Prince Charles, selfish if anyone had ever been, amoral, not intelligent enough to be moral, drifting about the moor of Culloden, while the Highlanders smashed themselves against that electronic fence, storming the enemy with their quick impetuous charges, while the enemy remained behind their guns, cool and collected. A business to them, an adventure to him.

I would have betrayed him if I had known, thought Martin, I would have sold him. He passed his hand across his brow and with a last look at the room went out into the lovely ambiguous April day.

On his way home he called in at a pub called the Crown, which he liked because it had secluded alcoves and large mirrors and usually a quiet atmosphere, and was just settling down with his whisky and lager when the large bearded writer Norman Maciver came in. Martin bought him a whisky and lager as well.

'And how are you, Martin?' said Norman, removing his sheepskin coat and throwing it over the leather seat. 'I hear you're going home, is that true?'

'It might be,' said Martin.

'You're a fool then. You're doing a good job here, and anyway what you're doing is important. You want to teach Gaelic in the Highlands. You can't have Gaelic without the backing of scholarship, can you? It would be absurd. Have you thought it through?' He quaffed his whisky in one draught and wiped his beard, which had traces of grey in it, and stared hard at Martin.

'Listen, can you imagine what the Gaelic world would be like without scholarship? It would be empty, there would be no depth to it. You're being a romantic fool. Anyone can teach; what you have is a highly specialised job for which you've been given a highly specialised training. Look at me. I want to write about the modern world as it is, as Highlanders here are experiencing it, and there are many of them in the cities too. It's true it would be better if I could do it at home, but at the same time I have to accept what has happened to us, it's what you might call a geographical infirmity. Come on, drink up. We have to put up with it, and that's all. I am writing a novel at the moment, a love story between a student who's been brought up in a strict Protestant atmosphere, and a Catholic girl. I'm finding it very interesting.'

'It's not that I'm against scholarship,' said Martin, swallowing his lager, 'it's that the crisis is so immediate. My God, I was trained to be a scholar, I like scholarship.'

'There you are then. I'll get another round. You

140

have no training in teaching younger people and it's very different from teaching older people, I can tell you. I started off by teaching, did you know that? I remember mentioning Pilate's name once in a class, and none of them had heard of him. And once after I had given what I thought was a very powerful lesson and had seen a girl staring at me as if absolutely riveted, she said to me, "Please, sir, where did you get your tie?" She had never seen a tartan tie before.'

Martin laughed.

'I come here quite often,' said Norman. 'Did you know the barman is from Skye? I bet you didn't know that. You've got the shyness of the true academic. And talking about academics, there was a book that was, I think, edited from your own university. It was a collection of Rob Donn's poetry; I was really influenced by that. I hadn't realised he was such a good poet. So you see there's that, and then you're training future teachers in scholarship. You're not in tune with pupils anyway, you'd be wasting your time. You're suffering from nostalgia, that's what's wrong with you, the Highland disease. If we don't get it from religion we get it from language. We should be sick of it by now.'

'I am sick of it,' said Martin. 'We're walking contradictions. They're sticking out of our backs.'

'Couldn't have put it better myself. People say that my children don't speak Gaelic. But what can I do about it, short of stopping their food, if they don't? The same problem is to be found among Pakistanis, Indians, here in Glasgow. Have you heard them talking with their perfect Glasgow accents? I heard one on the radio the other day, and when the interviewer asked him about his culture, and did he think it clashed with the Glasgow one,

141

he said, "No way." Listen, we have to have people like you in that university. And in any case I hear Jean doesn't want to go back. Is that right, old fellow?'

'It's right enough,' said Martin thoughtfully. 'Where did you hear that?'

'Oh, I met Nina. She's a great gossip. She stares out of her Glasgow tenement and wishes she was back home. And would she be any less lonely there, do you think? She's like the poetess Mairi Mhor nan Oran coming to Glasgow on the steamship, you know. My wife wouldn't go back, neither would my children. Is that a reason for feeling guilt? I can't drag them back, can I? I can have a job here, though it's not an awfully good one. Still, it allows me to write in the evenings.'

'But . . . '

'You're not convinced, of course. Of course not. It's like the toothache. It will always be with us. But what can we do? Come on, drink up. You're being a sentimental fool, if I may say it again.'

(And here I am drinking, thought Martin, and it's warm, and it's like those exiles who used to go to pubs in Canada because they were the only places where you could feel warm, with the snow and ice outside. And after a while the problems seem easy, as if lager and whisky could cure them.)

' . . . and it's not the same, not at all. You wouldn't know anyone now. One time I was home I was talking to this great footballer, an idol of my youth, and now he's an alcoholic and he kept saying to me, "But you're Norman Maciver, I hear you on the radio, you're different." It was heart-breaking, but what could be done about it? Did you bring your car?'

'No, I often walk to the university,' said Martin.

'Good, then that's no problem. My own one needs replacing but I can't afford to replace it at the moment.'

Martin got up and bought another whisky and lager. It occurred to him that they were drinking very fast, but he felt like drinking; he wasn't really a drinker and he hadn't been in a pub for a long time, and he thought perhaps he should phone Jean, but it was very comfortable where he was and he decided to stay. Anyway, it was refreshing to talk to Norman whose novels were quite good, using modern techniques in relation to new material.

'Look,' said Norman persuasively – his hair and beard are beginning to go grey, thought Martin, and he will wear the bottoms of his trousers rolled – 'there are many people who grow up in Yorkshire and never return to it. I'm just taking Yorkshire as an example. Or take D.H. Lawrence. He wandered the world; you can see that, can't you?'

'Yes, I can see that. But still . . . '

'You are asking me what use my novels are. I'll tell you. I write them from within my own world, my own language, but if I had stayed in the islands I would have been writing what had been written before. Now I'm writing something new. In my own way I'm extending the frontiers. Who will read me? I don't know. I'm not bothered. Do I make a living from it? No, I don't. How many novelists do?'

(If only a revelation would be given to me, thought Martin. If only I could unravel this problem which is making my head ache. So much talk . . . and if I could see it in the round, as if I were looking down on it, like a pilot sitting in his plane . . .)

' 'S bi ghealach toirt nam chuimhne-sa
liuthad oidhche bha sinn còmhla'

('And the moon brings back to my recollection
the many nights we were together')

Norman suddenly burst into song, making some
people at the bar turn and look at him, and then
turn away again back to their pints into which some
of them gazed with profound, questioning eyes.

'We are all attached to the homeland,' Norman
continued. 'I wonder why that is? Is there any other
race so attached? Come on, drink up. Can you tell
me a race more attached, eh?'

His leonine, grey-streaked head loomed out of
the mirror and his nose looked red as if he had
been drinking a lot recently.

'You know, the trouble with you', he said, pointing
a finger at Martin, 'is you don't have enough problems. You don't have a family. That's when you would
have problems. If you had a family you wouldn't have
time to think the way you do. Families are good for
academics, they drag them into the real world. You're
a comic figure, you're like the superfluous man in
Russian novels, you should be making meaningful
Russian noises, you should be doing heavy breathing
in Russian. Here's a point. You know at Christmas – I
hate Christmas – kids get a lot of presents, games and
stuff like that, and they ask me to teach them, but I
don't understand them myself. Do you see?'

And he staggered over to the bar where he got
another whisky and lager for both of them.

'Cluedo was one of them. I couldn't make head or
tail of it. Detective stuff going on in different rooms.
Tigh na galla. Eh? Who did what, eh?'

Martin told him about the incident with Calum

144

and he nearly rolled off his seat laughing, wiping his eyes with a large handkerchief which he took from his trouser pocket.

'Oh, just imagine it,' he said. 'The kilt. The fake dress. The direct hit. Like the Bismarck sinking. And Calum going down in the sunset. The *Téméraire*. I was at a *ceilidh* many years ago, and the chairman said, "We will now purvey the tea." I thought at first he said, "survey". And this woman straight up and down in her tartan rig, singing verse after verse of this interminable song.'

And he began to sing again

'Nuair a thèid mi gu Sràid Iamaica . . . '

('When I go to Jamaica Street')

'We're in a box, old boy. Joyce went to Europe to try silence, exile and cunning, but he wrote in English. If I try out exile and cunning who is going to read me, eh? But it's not a tragedy, old fellow. My parents died there the same as yours. I couldn't ask Brenda to take them down here. Yet my own mother looked after my grandmother for twenty years. She was a cantankerous old bag too. She used to tell my mother to beat me up.

'Oh, God, look who's coming! It's Morrison. And he's half seas over already. And he's seen us in the mirror. He's coming over.'

Morrison sat down beside them, laying his glass down carefully. His eyes flashed with a demonic glare, his little moustache seemed alive.

'My dear friends,' he said, sitting down, 'here we are gathered together in the sight of the barman. And how are you both? My friend here threw me out the other night,' he said, pointing to Martin. 'It was

145

a balmy night, otherwise I might have died. You're at the wake again discussing the corpse. Holding the wake.' He raised his glass mockingly. 'My friends, it was good while it lasted.'

At the far end of the bar a guitarist was beginning to tune up.

'Did you hear this one?' he asked Martin and Norman. 'There was this old man who stayed in what, shall we say, Uig, so this woman visitor, an American, perhaps with rinsed hair, came up to him while he was mending his net or whatever they do when they're not at church, and she said to him, "Mr Macritchie," shall we say he was called Macritchie, and Mr Macritchie, who in another existence was called Calum, said, "Yes, ma'am." "And is it true," said this woman, who was an existentialist from Texas, and who was wearing, shall we say, furs and a pre-Nixon hat, "is it true that you have a language here that you can use for any eventuality?" "Yes, ma'am," said Macritchie, whose pseudonym, as we have already said, was Calum, a cap-doffing peasant. "Very good," or "Wal I declare," said this woman, depending on whether she was from the Deep South or not, "And what would be the Gaelic for spaghetti bolognaise?" And Mr Macritchie, alias Calum, looked up at her with divine innocent eyes and said, "And what would be the English for it, ma'am?" Like it, eh?' And his small eyes glittered omnivorously.

'Very good,' said Norman. 'I see you didn't buy any of us a drink.'

'In a very short time, old fellow,' said Morrison. 'Very short. Cheques are beginning to bounce like the balls of my youth. And how is our spiritualist doing? Is he still yearning for Moscow? Ah, there is the distance beckoning.' And he began to sing,

' 'S daor a cheannaich mi an t-iasgach'

('Dearly did I pay for the fishing')

'Old Mackay there at the bar who is busy cleaning the glasses in case we all get Aids won't mind my singing. As a matter of fact, I've just come from another pub where I left a broadcaster or two looking for the Gaelic for National Health Service.' And he giggled into his beer.

'You're a bugger,' said Martin savagely. 'You never have any money. Why do you never have any money? Why do you never buy a round?'

'It's quite simple. I was reading an article the other day in which this learned man was saying that religion has nothing to do with the heavy incidence of drink in the islands. What a funny man. You think you're going to hell, but you take this as a matter of course, all that burning, etc, and gnashing of your neighbour's false teeth; it doesn't worry you, so you don't drink. Do you know, I heard this story the other day and it's absolutely true, there was a man I know from the Highlands who had a nervous breakdown and they had to ban his father from his bedside because he always came in with the Bible and said that his nervous breakdown had been caused by his lack of belief in burnt sheep and old prophets like Micah. Imagine that, eh? True story, absolutely.'

The guitarist, whose image they could now see reflected in the mirror, was a small man who wore a black hat, and had big moustaches like a Mexican. The light glittered from his guitar. He was beginning to sing, at first gently then more loudly, in an American drawl,

'that's what my mother told me . . . '

147

'The mother,' said Morrison. 'Have you ever thought of the concept of the mother in Gaelic and in Irish? The perfect one. The warm one. The one who will save us from the bruises of the day.

'Cha toir astar mòr a' chuain a gaol om' chridhe.'

('The great distance of the ocean will not remove her love from my heart.')

'The mother. We'll have to abolish her. Before we can grow up. We'll have to cut the apron strings once and for all.'

'Shut up,' said Martin and Norman in unison.

'Oh, I've touched a tender nerve, have I? It's true, my friends, nevertheless.'

'When I was just knee high.'

'By God, that guitarist looks furtive, doesn't he?'

Suddenly he got up and began to quarrel with the guitarist.

'Why do you sing in that American accent?' he shouted. 'That's not your accent, you don't normally talk like that.'

The guitarist withdrew from him nervously, holding his guitar close to him.

'It's an affectation,' Morrison was shouting at him. 'That's all it is. If you're going to sing that song you should sing it in your own accent.'

A large man appeared from somewhere in the region of the bar, took Morrison firmly by the arm and guided him in the direction of the door while Morrison shouted, 'It's all a lie, that's what it is.'

Then they heard no more; the large man spoke to

148

the guitarist, and the latter began to play and sing as before.

'Stupid clown!' said Martin angrily. 'Bloody stupid clown.'

He was beginning to feel slightly drunk, and thought that he should go home, but he felt too comfortable.

'Jean told me the other day that she would go to Raws with me after all,' he told Norman.

'Oh?'

'She said she had changed her mind since it meant so much to me.'

'And?'

'I said I would think about it. This is the drunkest I've been for a long time. It reminds me of the time when I was a student in Aberdeen. I was drinking and I returned for the dance at the Union, and I was sick all over this green shoe. It was a woman who was wearing it. I looked up and there she was, looking down at me, while my vomit was all over her green shoe.'

He lifted his head, vaguely hearing a harsh raucous voice that he recognised. It was from the TV.

'That's that bugger, Paisley,' he said. 'Are you hearing him? Listen.'

The voice, unforgiving and gravelly, was saying that Ulster would never surrender to the Anglo-Irish Agreement, never, never, never. Ulster would fight to the last drop of blood before it would submit to being Irish. Its flag was the UK flag; it had fought for the UK in the war, it had sent its sons to foreign fields, only the UK conveniently forgot that now. Its flag and its soil were sacred. Brutal and righteous, the voice drowned out the piteous questions of the interviewer; it was like a huge hammer falling on very delicate wood.

'Bastard!' Martin shouted. 'Self-righteous bastard. He never thinks there could be another side to the problem.'

'It's the dream, you see,' said Norman quietly. 'It's the terrible dream.'

'What did you say?'

'The dream. A babbled o'green fields. Though green is perhaps not the right word for Paisley. Have you heard their songs? I have. Their ballads. The UDR heroes who fight for Ulster. You see it everywhere, the dream. For the dream isn't rational. That's why you can't beat the dream, you aren't dealing with reason. It was the same when Kennedy met Khrushchev, who was the Paisley of Russia. Kennedy, the liberal, met the dream and was nearly destroyed by it. And it all led to the Cuban crisis. Don't you remember? Or maybe you are too young.'

'What is this dream you're talking about?' said Martin angrily, spilling some of his beer as he raised it to his lips.

'You see it everywhere now, the irrational dream. Terrorists have it, the Jews have it, Ulster has it. The dream of the child who must have everything, who doesn't negotiate with reality. The child who screams and demands instant obedience, instant relief. The little giant who shouts, Give me, give me. I will have all or nothing. And all things are possible to the dream. It has its flags and its tremendous colour and its marches. The sleep of reason breeds monsters. Did you never hear that? It was Goya who said that. Who can talk to the dreamer? Politics was once the art of the possible, now the impossible is being demanded instantly. Can you not hear it in Paisley's voice, the scream of the unappeasable child?'

Martin felt himself almost falling asleep. Now and again, he would shake his head like a dog coming out of the sea, freeing itself of water.

'There was once', he said, 'in the village a very, very fat woman. I don't think she was all there. Her legs were bare, and raw and fat, and her skirt was so short that she looked grotesque. She wandered about the village talking to herself, and she kept a lot of cats. We boys used to throw stones at her door and when she came to the door we hid behind her house. I remember it was quite near a well. She died among her cats.'

He glared angrily at Norman. 'What a shower of little buggers we were. Cruel little bastards. What were you trying to say to me there? You're a devious bastard. I forgot what you were trying to say.'

And he slapped Norman on the shoulder. 'You look like a Russian yourself with that beard. You look like a member of the Orthodox Church.'

'Hadn't we better be going?' said Norman.

'Not at all, not at all. You're my guru. You have wisdom to give me. I feel it. Your beard testifies to it. In the old days it was only old men who wore beards, now it is only young men who wear them. You never see an old man with a beard now except a Jew, perhaps a Jew. What have you to say to that, guru?'

'Listen,' said Norman to him, 'you're in danger. I can see it.'

'Danger? How do you mean, danger? What are you talking about? What are you having?'

'I've had enough.'

'All right, then. Explain yourself. What do you mean, danger?'

151

'There's a saying that the Highlander doesn't understand his loss till it happens to him.'

'And what does that mean, guru?'

'Just that you might lose Jean and then . . . you'll be alone. You've never been alone, have you?'

'Alone? No, I've never been alone.'

'Well, then, don't be dismissive about it. I've been alone. And I know what it's like. I don't think you're the sort of person who would easily live alone. I'm just telling you.'

'Yes, O guru. I'm listening.'

'I don't think you are. I don't think you're listening at all. Anyway, I have to go. I hope you're going home as well.'

'I'm going to the bog first.'

'See you then.'

And Norman left him.

For a while he sat there and then got up rather unsteadily and made his way to the toilet. He swayed on his feet as he peed steadily into the drain along which floated fragments of cigarettes. The walls were crowded with graffiti like a medieval manuscript.

When he had finished he made his way out, but as he did so he noticed that there was a fish tank brightly illuminated in a corner near the door. He stopped and looked at it. After a while it was as if he were hypnotised by the restless circuits of the fish in their lighted world.

Staring owlishly into the tank, he followed the progress of one fish larger than the others. Its constant motion was an enigma and an inspiration to him. The hair on his head almost stood on end. He knew that this was a moment of tremendous import to him. There swam into his mind the image of Jean's almost unknown father, drifting about in ignorant seas, for ever and for ever. The ceaseless energy of the fish confined in their glaring yet mysterious box puzzled him, and the bubbles enchanted him as if he were a child again. Life, life, contemporary life, in its box on which its own sun shone, green and strange. And that body floating, but once alive, joining another one in a flash of spectacular energy.

It took him a great effort to wrench himself away from the greenish box and to turn unsteadily to the door, the image remaining with him, not wholly rational, not wholly grasped, unparaphrasable, mysterious, doomed, restless, played upon by the unsleeping light.

All the way home he was looking inside the box. It was as if he were carrying it with him as he once used to carry the water from the well in a bucket, very carefully, lest he should spill any of it. Its greenish light was not eerie, rather it was natural and vibrant with energy. Its sun was not of another world but of this world. Its constant movement delighted him as if it were a new toy that he had been given by pure chance. It reminded him of staring into sea water in his childhood, the soupy pools that could be found at the back of the stone pier in his village. Nor was it only that hapless body drifting about that he saw, he saw also his father, his mother, and himself and Jean.

But also he saw it as an explosion of seed, of chromosomes, of genes. He staggered and swayed, as if he were a drunk, carrying the phantom box in his mind. Sometimes he could see Jean peering into it as if it were a jewellery box in which she kept the few personal ornaments that she had. And he saw

153

her, a bewildered orphan, in the house in which she grew up. She was looking into a mirror; her dark hair was long and glossy. It was long before she met him; she was however searching the mirror for her future husband. Her face was hopeful and clear.

He stopped and leaned against a wall. He wanted to weep, but at the same time he could see himself as a typical weeping drunk and this disgusted him. Soon, if he continued like this, he would stop the next person he saw and tell them his life history. Lishen, he would say, no one undershtans me. And he would take out a huge dirty handkerchief and wipe his face with it. Lishen, there wash . . . there wash . . . Shee my box.

Nina drifted towards him. She was saying, I spent my life knitting and looking out the window. Imagine that. I dreamed of a green place, but I stayed here, reading the streets. The streets were my manuscripts, my favourite writing. I was so alone. And someone else was singing a song from a room in a tenement near him.

He staggered in front of a bus, and the driver shouted at him. He waved his hand feebly and found himself on the other side of the street. He began to laugh as he thought of a story. There was a man peeing in a toilet, a drunk man, and he saw a half-smoked cigarette drifting past in the drain. He put it in his mouth and tried to smoke it. There was a toff in a top hat and white collar standing beside him peeing as well.

Lishen, he said to the toff, ever shmoked a chigar you found in a toilet?

No, said the toff, can't say I have.

Well, said the drunk, Itsh no very good, I can tell you that. He stopped, and laughed and laughed.

154

A young girl looked at him and passed on. Itsh no very good, he said to the green box.

He looked up into the sky. There was a moon, bone white and fragmentary, like a piece of peel, high above him. It's the same moon as is shining over Raws, he thought. And this reminded him again of his student days, irresponsible and delightful. The moon of the harvest, it will take us home to the islands.

Then he began to think of the vase with the picture of Orpheus and Eurydice on it. There was dim darkness, and the mineral king sat among his treasures. Orpheus played his guitar, clad in his white classical dress, and the king granted his wish. Orpheus however looked back from the rim of earth and the ghostly Eurydice disappeared. Why had he looked back? Had he decided at that moment that there was no going back, that he was finished with that darkness, these treasures, that he must go forward into what Martin imagined as an April day, shuttling with sun and shadow?

He thought of the moon above him, this time not fragmentary but round and full, a disembodied head, a head of the intellect alone.

The city lay in front of him. All things were possible to it; strangers who were important to one might appear round the corner at any moment. Marvellous meetings were available, collisions, epiphanies. The city was a labyrinth of opportunity, creative, fecund.

And so he arrived eventually at his house. It was nearly midnight.

★

Jean was still waiting up for him.

'Where have you been?' she asked.

'I was in a pub. I met Norman Maciver. We had long philosophical discussions.'

'It looks like it.'

'I thought of many things. About your mother and father, for instance.'

'Oh?'

'Uh, huh. And about my own mother and father. By the way, do we have any black coffee?'

'I'm sure I could arrange it.'

'Good, good,' said Martin absently. 'I haven't felt as drunk as this for a long time.'

'Do you want to go to bed then?'

'No, not at all. In wine is wisdom, as some philosopher from Raws once said. I walked under the moon and it reminded me of my youth. Nights of wine and neuroses. It's odd. There were times when I was frightened and nervous then. Especially before examinations.'

She set a mug of black coffee before him on the scrubbed table.

'It occurred to me that you knew loneliness more than I have ever known it. Isn't that right?'

'I suppose it is.'

'When you were growing up, I mean. You must have been lonely. It's something Norman said. And then there was Orpheus. When he climbed upward to the sky he must have felt loneliness. He must have decided on it and tried the new air.'

'I don't know what you're talking about.'

'The communal shades or the individuality. The communal shades muttering and gossiping. Whispering.'

'What *are* you going on about?'

'Jean, did you dream when you were young?'

'Of course I did. Everybody dreams.'

'What were your dreams?'

'My dreams? I dreamed that my father was a sea-captain. I once told my teacher that. I wrote a composition about it. We used to call them compositions in those days. I had an idea that he was the captain of the ship in which he sank. Of course he wasn't. He was just an ordinary sailor. I also thought of him as handsome. When I later saw the photograph of him he wasn't handsome at all. I thought he looked rather stout. I had made drawings of him and he looked like a prince in them. I even gave him a moustache.'

'Yes, I understand. It's a funny thing, but my father and mother used to quarrel more than I later remembered. There was one quarrel in particular which went on and on. My mother wanted a new door and my father said that we didn't need it. He was very careful with money. She had gone into town and had seen this door and she wanted it. 'The house is all right as it is,' he would say. 'What do you want a new door for?'

'I used to draw him with crayons,' said Jean, smiling. 'I knew enough to give him a navy blue uniform but I also gave him a gold cap. Of course, the teacher who was local knew that he wasn't a captain. Drink your coffee.'

'Oh, I'm sorry. And there was another time when my father gave me hell. For some reason he was teaching me to make knots, complicated knots, and I couldn't get them right. He was quite abrupt and hot-tempered at times. He had a straw-coloured moustache.'

'I never saw him.'

157

'And I never saw either your father or your mother. Did you not like your aunt at all?'

'She was very religious. So was my uncle. She was very strict. She didn't want the same thing to happen to me as had happened to my mother. I think she was quite fond of my mother in her own way. She was older than my mother.'

'She was trying to protect you?'

'I don't know. Perhaps she was. I remember she had something wrong with her once and she wouldn't go to the doctor. I think it was shame or shyness that prevented her from going.'

'But she was trying to protect you?'

'I don't know why you go on about that. Perhaps she was. I don't know. She had a funny way of doing it. She was always saying, "You don't have any gratitude."'

'And did you?'

'I don't know. I was very young. She would never let me go to a dance. Dancing was sinful.'

'Yes, of course. I remember my father once went to the school and said he didn't want me to take French. He was very argumentative. "I don't want my son to take French," he shouted. "What does he want French for?" And then he went on about the war.'

'Did you take French then?'

'I took Gaelic. I was quite ashamed that day. I could have curled up and died. Memories.'

'What do you mean?'

'What we choose to forget and remember. And then of course you took that job in a travel agent's and before that in a hotel. You wanted to travel.'

'I did travel.'

'Of course. That was why you took the job.'

'I remember when I was in Germany thinking I might send my aunt a postcard but I decided against it. I had just come out of the cathedral in Cologne and I thought of sending her a postcard of it, but I didn't.'

'The cathedral?'

'Anyway, I didn't send it. I felt so free. I loved these churches and cathedrals. There was one in particular and there was a statue of the Virgin Mary. In simple blue. And she was holding her child out as if she was offering it. This made a deep impression on me. It was a very simple likeness, sea-blue.'

'Did your aunt and uncle have any children?'

'No. That was why they took me.'

'What were you doing tonight?'

'Nothing much. I did an ironing. I thought you might be in a pub. Or teaching that girl? Your pseudo-daughter.'

'No, I was in a pub. Anyway, her mother is leaving. She decided that since her daughter didn't have any money and had run away she must start earning some. She told me she had this dream of going to the Highlands. But then she decided that her daughter might not like it anyway. So they're leaving.'

'Where will they go?'

'Where she will find a job. It's not easy to find a job though.'

'No, I suppose not. So you went to the pub after that.'

'I did. And there I met Norman Maciver and also Morrison who was thrown out for verbally slanging the guitar player because he sang in a pseudo-American accent. Idiot. But you like him, don't you?'

'I can't stand him.'

'I feel the better for that coffee,' said Martin. 'I feel human. When I was walking home I could see myself as a drunk. I remember once when I was coming home on the bus on the island I and another fellow got off for a pee. There were a lot of flowery bushes about. And this fellow was drunk to the eyeballs and he kept singing over and over something about Sauchiehall Street as he peed into the bushes. There was a moon that night as well. And there was a strong scent from the bushes.'

'Sauchiehall Street?'

'I think it was Sauchiehall Street. And then he wanted to fight me. Because I was a student. "Bloody scholar," he kept saying over and over as he swayed and peed among the bushes. And another thing came into my head just now.'

'What was that?'

'Oh, it was a friend of my father's. He had been in Canada and America in his youth, probably went over on the *Metagama*, I don't know, or maybe later. Used to do salmon fishing and work in the grain elevators. For years after he came home he used to go down and watch the mail boat come in. One day, this was in the town, myself and my father were talking to him. And he said he should never have come home. "I should have stayed in Canada," he kept saying. We were out in his garden where he had some potatoes and cabbages and things like that. And he kept saying, "I should never have come home. Greatest mistake of my life." As a matter of fact I heard he used to drink heavily when he was in Canada; and for a while after he came home he was a bit of a tramp. Then he started going to church and he married this very pious woman who sat in a chair like a Buddha and smiled

160

and smiled. Well, after we had been out for a while it started getting chilly and we went into the house. He had an old dog that lay by the fire and dozed. When he came in he began to shout at the dog. "You never go anywhere!" he shouted all of a sudden. "You just stay around the house." And he gave it a tremendous kick. And it yelped, and ran and hid behind the sofa. Then he opened his newspaper and began to read it.'

There was a silence for a while.

'Funny how these things come back to me tonight. As if I could see much more clearly than usual.'

He and Jean were sitting on opposite sides of the scrubbed table in the kitchen. He suddenly thought of it as a negotiating table in the bright light which poured on it. The kitchen itself was very large, with cupboards of the same wood as the table, a light oak which was beginning to have autumnal tints.

'I forgot to tell you I saw Calum today,' said Jean. 'He told me that Nina was ill.'

'I'm sorry to hear that.'

'He had been to visit her. He's got a kind heart, Calum. Of course he's known Nina most of her life.'

'What's wrong with her?'

'I think it's cancer.'

'Oh, my God.'

'Yes, indeed. She's in hospital.'

'And all those years she saw the island and she never saw Glasgow. Sitting at her window knitting.'

'As a matter of fact I had a long talk with Calum. Did you know that her husband, who was a policeman, had an affair with some woman in Glasgow for many years? Calum said that he was a bit of a womaniser.'

'No, I didn't know that.'

'Very handsome man, Calum said. In fact it started

161

before Nina and him came to Glasgow. He would stay with this woman and then go and stay with Nina in the summer months. Then Nina decided that she would come to Glasgow. But he didn't stop seeing her till a few years before he died.'

'I didn't know any of this,' said Martin wonderingly.

'Calum knows everything about the expatriates. The exiles, as he calls them. You didn't know that at one time Nina was thinking of buying a hotel? She worked very hard as a receptionist when she came to Glasgow and she saved up all her money. But nothing came of it. She's actually a very capable woman, according to Calum, and, at one time, secretary of the committee.'

'Well, I'm damned,' said Martin, pouring himself another cup of coffee. 'Do you want any?'

'No, thanks. We'll have to go and see her. She's in the Western Infirmary. I could get her some heather. She might like that.'

'No,' said Martin suddenly. 'Not at all. We won't get her any heather.'

'Well, she won't be allowed any vodka.'

'Oh, I wasn't thinking of that. Something else, but not heather. I've a feeling she won't last long anyway.'

'Why do you say that?'

'I just have a feeling about her. I'm sorry to hear about that,' he said again. 'And what about Calum himself? Has he recovered?'

'Oh, I think so. He has his own troubles, I believe. He would like to go to the island for a holiday, but his wife won't go. She's apparently a difficult woman. Very conscious of her own importance at functions too. Calum isn't really like that.'

'No, I don't suppose he is. I believe he's a very kind man.'

'This has nothing to do with what we were talking about,' said Jean, staring down at the table, 'but do you remember that day in the art gallery when we met, why did you speak to me and then ask me out?'

'I don't know. I suppose it was because I felt lonely.'

'*You* felt lonely?'

'Why else do you think I went to the art gallery? As you know, I never make friends easily. And then you were looking at that painting: it was, I think, the *Misanthrope*. I suppose it was the contrast between you and the painting. I never found it easy to make friends with girls. We had lots of quarrels in those days, do you remember? You were very difficult. Sometimes you would shout and scream at me.'

'But we always made up.'

'Yes, I used to bring you huge bouquets of flowers. You thought of me as the one who deserted you, your mother. You were very insecure.'

'There was something cold about you then as well. You loved your books. You didn't want to talk to me much. Sometimes it was as if I was in your way.'

'I was always used to silence,' said Martin thoughtfully. 'That's what it was. And then I had to learn not to be so used to silence. Do you think marriage is always like that, negotiations must take place?'

'What do you mean, negotiations?'

'Like the dream. Negotiations between the dreams. This was what Norman said to me tonight. Someone has to sit down at a bare table like this in the light of reality and negotiate. Set the limits. You see it was nothing to do with Raws at all, nothing to do with going back there. You were right enough in your instinctive reaction at the beginning. It has to do with

163

us, not with Raws. It all has to do with growing up. You see, what we tend to forget when we talk about the island is that it is our childhood we are talking about. We are confusing childhood with idealism, I think. Or in your case non-idealism.'

He got up and walked about the kitchen as if to get it right. Through the window he could see the fractured moon, a sliver in the sky.

'It occurred to me tonight that I'm always talking about my university days, and often thinking about them. That's because they were totally irresponsible. And I met so many dreamers there too . . . A fellow who used to go about in a long black coat like some sort of a vampire. Poseurs of all kinds. Dreamers. Do you know a story that I would like to write, except that I'm not creative? I would go back to Aberdeen as I am now and I would meet my younger self. He would be with a lot of other students. There would probably be a moon overhead. Either he would not recognise me at all and pass me, or he would feel contempt for me. Or I would draw attention to who I was. And he would say, "Is that all you've become? I had such high hopes of you. And you were only human after all. Why, you've even got a paunch." Or he would be so bright, so unrelentingly bright that he would annihilate me. I think perhaps I would plead with him and he would be so aloof, so aristocratic, there would be no pity in him at all. "So there you are," he would say, "purveying tea, after all my great expectations." And he would also be very theatrical. I think of him as swinging a cane. And that moon shining overhead. When we're young we make a lot of the moon. Later, we lose it altogether.'

He went and sat down at the bare table again.

'We're like drunks, we have such expectations.

We talk of what might be possible, of the prizes we might win, spending money we haven't got.'

He felt inspired, as if all was at last clear, while Jean was gazing at him, as if she couldn't believe in his garrulity.

'At first,' she said, 'when I used to come home from my work, I'd have all sorts of stories and you wouldn't listen to them. You didn't think them important. I stored them up for you, and after a while I didn't bother because you weren't listening to me. Literally, you didn't listen to me. And there were strange stories. Like the couple who misread the instructions in their room in Spain and it said that they must vacate their room at twelve o'clock noon, so they used to take their stuff down to the beach every day after twelve o'clock and bring it back in the evening. I used to think that was a great story, but you never listened to me. It was as if you were listening to someone else, to some other story, but never to mine.'

'That's true,' he said. 'That's what happened.'

'Do you know,' she said, 'when I was convinced that you would leave I wondered where I would go, and then Daphne said I could move in with her.'

'Daphne?'

'One of the girls I work with.'

'You mean you seriously thought . . . ?'

'I had to work it out. I would be alone, you see. I had to think of what would happen. Did you not think of what would happen?'

'You mean you told her?'

'Of course I told her. I had to tell someone.'

'I never thought you would tell anyone,' said Martin quietly. 'It never occurred to me to tell anyone.'

165

'That's because you have your books. People like us have to live from day to day, that's what you don't seem to understand. We have to feed on what is available. We have to peck and peck.'

He stared at her. 'I never thought of that before.'

'You didn't know how lucky you were, I used to think,' said Jean. 'You had an aim. I had to phone . . . make plane appointments for people. That was my work. And before that I had to fit people into rooms. But you had important work, and you didn't know it. You were like a child. I thought you were being childish.'

'Yes,' he said, 'that's what it is. The dream. There was that play and they were blundering about the wood, all dreaming. And the Duke came along in the cold light of morning, the dew on his boots, and said to them that they must listen to reason. They had all been following the moon, they were all moonstruck.'

The moon of the harvest, the moon that brings us home to Raws . . .

The moon of the dream, the red moon of the dream, the vampire moon, the moon that sucks our blood.

Without thinking, he went and pulled the curtains to block it out, that thin fragment that floated on the edge of the sky. There were only the two of them in the kitchen. He had wanted to bring his mother down here. That too was part of the dream. And Jean had known that instinctively. He had tried to pull his mother into his dream whereas she wouldn't have existed in that reality which was not for her a dream. Like the Trojan carrying his aged father on his back. But it would never have worked, and Jean had been right.

Like ships in the night. We pass each other like ships in the night, our dreams blazing. And we don't see each other.

And he looked at Jean. Her face looked pale and there were shadows under her eyes, as if she hadn't been sleeping well. He noticed that she was nervously picking at a single fork that had been lying on the table, now and again idly pushing the prongs into the palm of her hand.

And another story came into his head. It was one Nina had told him. A friend of hers was suffering from senile dementia, and didn't recognise her own husband. She would say, 'Who are you? I want to leave this house. I don't know this house.' And she would try to pack her things and leave. Then she would talk about her husband as if he wasn't there, and sometimes she would say, 'Who was that child I heard crying in the night? We must find that child.' Her husband, who had been a seaman, used to make models of ships which he put in bottles and the wife would look at the ship for hours. The only pleasure she got was from the ship models.

We are privileged, thought Martin, we are privileged to be together. Beyond everything, beneath everything, is that loneliness which I didn't understand. But we are privileged to be together. Imagine the possibilities that the imagination can create – that she does not understand me, that she strokes the ship in the bottle, that she is crying for the nameless child lost somewhere in this house.

We must wrench the dream from our hearts.

This is the bare negotiating table of reality. We are sitting at it now. He knew he would never go back, that the fever was over.

'Come on,' he said, 'it's time to go to bed.'

167

They climbed the stairs together. Later, he watched the moon through the window. It was a small fragment, nothing like the blaze it had once been. It was like the fractured rind of a fruit.

He thought idly before he fell asleep that if it had been a full moon he might have seen it as a ball that had flown idly over a fence and he would have gone to ask for his ball back.

Smiling, he fell asleep, at first rocking with the dregs of the drink, and then settling down. He hardly ever dreamed in his sleep and tonight was no exception.